DEATH OF
A
PREACHER
MAN

**Second century AD,
under the reign of Emperor Hadrian**

The legionary camp of *Vindobona* is located on the southern bank of the Danubius River, as part of the Limes that secures the borders of the Roman Empire. It is flanked by two insignificant civilian settlements and sits on the very spot where the city of Vienna will blossom in the distant future.

The inhabitants are Celts, Germanic tribes and Roman citizens, and the soldiers of the legionary camp are recruited from almost every corner of the Empire.

Only recently, some of the town's most respected residents have fallen victim to a series of terrible murders. But now a new, much worse threat is brewing in the house of the Germanic merchant Thanar....

I

The disaster had its beginning on a bitterly cold evening, shortly before the Ides of the twelfth month. Or at any rate, it found its way into my house at that time.

The night was without moon or stars, as dark as one would imagine the deepest abyss of the underworld to be. The first snowflakes were falling outside the windows.

I had made myself comfortable along with my two guests in the pleasantly heated triclinium, my Roman-style dining room. The tribune Titus Granius Marcellus was lying opposite me, and Layla was stretched out at his side. As hard as I tried, I couldn't take my eyes off her. Until a few months before, she had been my slave—and my lover.

But perhaps I should first introduce myself, before I tell you about my beloved: my name is Thanar, and I think I can say, with all modesty, that I am one of the most respected merchants in Vindobona. My beginnings were, well, less than glorious, but that doesn't matter in terms of the account I want to give here, for this my chronicle of the terrible events that chose my house as their scene.

I deal in amber, the gold of the north, furs, silverware, jewels and works of art, and almost all the other treasures the world has to offer.

I used to travel a lot to further my business. Lately, however, I have placed these arduous and dangerous undertakings in the hands of my servants, first and foremost those of

Darius, my assistant, whom I trust unconditionally. He has run my business to my complete satisfaction and in the last few months has generated profits that have dwarfed all my previous earnings. So I was doing excellently—financially speaking.

The property I call home is located north of the Danubius River, which forms the Limes of the Roman Empire—that border fortified with numerous legionary camps and watchtowers, which for the Romans represents the northern edge of the civilized world.

I belong to one of those peoples who are summarized by the Romans under the term *Germanic tribes*. In truth, we are a handful of independent and sometimes quite hostile peoples that share certain commonalities, just like our southern and western neighbors, who are called *Celts* by the Romans in the same generalized way. These vague collective terms are fully sufficient for the mentally lazy citizens of the Imperium Romanum.

For the uneducated Roman, we and the Celts are even one and the same: simply, barbarians.

But again, this doesn't matter in terms of my report. I should really try not to digress so much right at the beginning.

Marcellus had come unexpectedly to my house on that frosty winter evening, together with Layla, who was now his lover and no longer mine. Of all things, in the midst of that cruel series of murders in which all three of us had been involved a few months ago, he had fallen in love with my beautiful slave. And I—who thought of myself as an intelligent and worldly man—had not noticed anything until the end.

After I had turned Layla from a slave into a *liberta*, a freedwoman, she had asked me to let her continue living under my roof as part of my familia, as is quite usual for freed slaves. Her room, located right next to mine, had been available for her at any time since then.

I had furnished it even more beautifully and luxuriously, with an ornate ivory couch, a precious carpet, and many other amenities.

However, Layla in fact hardly stayed under my roof more than a few days a month. The rest of the time she spent in the tribune house of Marcellus, in the legionary camp of Vindobona.

That is, lately in the legate palace of Marcellus, because he had been promoted. In my mind, he was still Tribune Marcellus. But that was wrong. *Legate* Marcellus was now the correct form of address. Legion X Gemina, which was stationed in Vindobona, was now under his supreme command.

It was not the career move itself that surprised me. Marcellus was young, barely past twenty, but he was a very capable and ambitious man, and a born leader. Moreover, he came from an influential noble Roman family.

No, what surprised me was that he had sought the position of legionary commander of Vindobona at all.

The usual career for a man of his standing would have included a year or two as tribune at Vindobona, followed by a new, similar assignment elsewhere in the Empire, and finally, as soon as was feasible, an influential position in Rome itself—or at least in an important city of the Empire. Vindobona can truly not be called such.

I love my homeland, but from the point of view of a Roman nobleman, it is merely a forgotten provincial nest at the end of the world.

I knew what kept Marcellus in Vindobona, though: Layla. He was still here because of her. She didn't want to leave our province, although I couldn't figure out what was keeping her here. Was it me, as I told myself in my most hopeful moments?

Did Marcellus really love her so much that he would put his political career on the back burner for her? It was possible; I would have done the same myself.

I can certainly call Marcellus a good friend, even though he has stolen my beloved. I appreciate his cleverness, and his courage, with which he has already saved my life once. And I must admit that he is much better suited to Layla than I am. He is an attractive young man and right in Layla's age group. I, on the other hand, am already approaching forty and, although I consider myself presentable, I am not such a beau as Marcellus.

When the young legate was lying next to Layla, as he was right now in my dining room, they made a wonderful couple. Both of their hair was night-black, as were their eyes. Both were of slender, very pleasing figure. Marcellus, however, had the fair complexion of a Roman, while Layla came from Nubia and was dark-skinned like a black Sphinx.

Of course, it was impossible for the scion of a respectable noble Roman family to marry a freedwoman, but Marcellus seemed to love Layla sincerely. She, on the other hand, never told me anything about her feelings. Not about Marcellus, nor about whether and what she still felt for me. In any case, she seemed to have no ambitions to persuade Marcellus in any way to marry her, which gave me hope. I hadn't given up on her yet, even if I had no idea how I was going to win back her heart.

II

During dinner, Marcellus had said not a word about what had brought him to my house tonight. I could see that something was on his mind, but he had dined with unusual taciturnity.

Meanwhile, Layla had engaged in polite conversation with me. She had praised the comfort of my dining room, the exquisite taste of the food ... and now she was raving with great enthusiasm about the Greek statue that I had recently added to the room. It was a life-size image of a female flute player, carved by a master's hand from the finest marble. I estimated the age of the sculpture at over three hundred years. Of its former, certainly magnificent colored coat, only tiny remnants had survived in some grooves, but the blank white marble appealed to me. So I had decided not to have the statue restored.

Layla had come to my house tonight wrapped in a precious fur. Underneath, she wore a robe of white silk, in which she now lay at the table, and which formed a wonderful contrast to her black skin. Her hair was piled up in a complicated hairstyle, and around her neck was a beautiful pearl necklace. Surely all these luxuries were gifts from Marcellus. Layla looked like a queen, not a freedwoman. And yet her nature had not changed a bit. She was still the gentle and modest girl I knew and loved. And the mind that hid behind her charming exterior was as sharp as ever.

Marcellus cleaned his fingertips in a bowl of water that one of my servants handed him. Then he cleared his throat and leaned forward.

"I want your advice, Thanar," he began in a deliberate tone. His youthful brow was deeply furrowed, and his voice sounded as if it belonged to a veteran of the legion who had fought on all too many battlefields.

"Is there trouble with Paulus again?" I ventured a guess.

Marcellus nodded, barely noticeable. "You could say that. If he goes on like this, I'll have an uprising on my hands soon. Every day more influential citizens of the city address me and implore me to put an end to the outrage. They fear the vengeance of the gods—and probably not without good reason."

Iulius Paulus was the argentarius of Vindobona. He exchanged money, kept silver and gold for a fee, and granted loans at halfway acceptable interest rates. I knew him well. In my early days as a merchant, I had often borrowed money from him, but now I only occasionally exchanged coins at his shop.

But Paulus's business as argentarius had faded into the background. In recent months, he had transformed himself from a bustling businessman into a preacher and prophet proclaiming to the inhabitants of Vindobona that the end was near; the Day of Judgment, as he called it. The apocalypse, followed by the kingdom of his god on earth. Paulus had become a fanatical follower of those cultists who called themselves Christians. He referred to himself as an apostle—a messenger of God who was spreading the true faith.

Paulus was a few years older than me, but was still in

excellent health. In the past, he had been quite fond of the pleasures of *luxuria*. He had enjoyed watching an exciting gladiatorial fight in the amphitheater just as much as lazing around in the thermal baths. And he had never spurned a good meal. That was over now; his highest aspirations had changed to renunciation and asceticism.

Under the name Paulus he had already been known as argentarius, but now this name had a whole new meaning for him. It filled him with pride that he was called after his great role model, the apostle Paulus of Tarsus, of whom he spoke constantly.

If I understood correctly, that man had once been an avowed enemy of the Christians, but then a divine vision had thrown him off his horse on the road to Damascus. And Paulus of Tarsus had become one of the most important apostles of the new cult.

I had already met these so-called Christians on one or another trade trip. They were militant atheists who denied all gods except their own. Terrible things were said about them—that they committed incest, that they indulged in depraved rituals, even sacrificing babies at their secret meetings. And the worst of all: that they were cannibals.

And the Christians were out to win new converts for their god. They always followed the same pattern: they approached you in the marketplace, in the forum, quite innocently at first. As if they wanted to be your friend. But then they suddenly began to tell you about their strange god, who was the most powerful, no, the only true one—but who had allowed the Romans to crucify his son. That seemed to be no contradiction for the Christians. Jesus had sacrificed himself for us humans, they claimed. Which was quite the wrong way around, in my humble opinion; people sacrificed to the gods, not vice versa.

Moreover, each of these fanatics I'd met on my travels told a slightly different story about Jesus, his deeds and his death. The Christians argued among themselves about what the true teaching was. I guess they didn't really know themselves what they believed, and yet they wanted to convert others.

Wherever they appeared, they caused bad blood among the population. They called all gods—except their own—false idols or worse, demons. They even refused to offer sacrifices to the Roman emperors who have ascended to the heaven of the gods after death.

It angers the gods if they are not shown the necessary respect. For this reason, the Christians are hated by the people, and they have been blamed for all the evils that can befall a city. However, I also had the impression that these strange cultists preferred to die rather than renounce their faith. Becoming a martyr seemed to be a Christian's highest aspiration and promise of happiness.

On the other hand, Jesus' followers also did good things. They healed the sick, cast out demons, and they were able to get their god to work amazing miracles. So maybe he did have great power, as they claimed?

I myself have not yet reached a conclusion about it. Before our argentarius in Vindobona had become the apostle of the Christian god, I had not really thought about this new cult.

Paulus had already healed the possessed and saved the terminally ill from death in Vindobona, it was said. Moreover, he was a respected—and quite wealthy—Roman citizen. So Marcellus could not simply expel him from the town, even though Paulus was causing growing unrest in Vindobona and invoking the wrath of the gods upon us all.

"Do you think all the atrocities told about these Christians are true?" I asked Marcellus, while one of my servants re-filled our cups.

"That they practice incest?" asked the legate. "And that they eat people?"

I nodded.

Marcellus brushed a strand of his dark hair from his face and sighed. "I don't know. In any case, this Jesus, the prophet to whom they pay homage, already was a rebel. I have made inquiries. How on earth can a criminal who died in shame on the cross be worshipped as a god?" He shook his head, uncomprehendingly.

Then he reached for his freshly filled wine cup and took a big gulp. "Paulus, however, is not the reason I seek you out, my friend. I can handle him on my own, I swear."

My curiosity was aroused.

"The matter at issue—" Marcellus hesitated for a moment, seemingly undecided about how to express himself, which was a very uncharacteristic behavior for him. He was not otherwise the thoughtful type, in the habit of weighing his words. In general, he expressed his mind clearly and di-rectly, even at the risk of offending his audience.

He gave Layla a look that I could not interpret. Then he continued, "A guest has come to me, Thanar, a Celtic noble-woman. Divicia is her name, and the reason for her visit—" Again he fell silent, rubbing the bridge of his nose with his thumb and forefinger, and took another sip of wine.

Then he said, "Her appearance may be a ray of hope as far as Paulus is concerned. But it may also exacerbate our problems; I can't gauge that yet."

I gestured impatiently for him to continue.

"I met Divicia shortly after I came to Vindobona, this spring. I was on the road with some legionaries, here on the Danubius's northern shore. Acquainting myself with the area, you know. That's when she crossed my path with a group of Celtic warriors. I recognized right away that Divicia belonged to the nobility. She is … a majestic woman. Yes, I think you have to say that."

This time it was Layla who gave him a long glance; one of her cryptic looks, which I was never able to interpret, and which made her look like the famous Sphinx. Inscrutable and mysterious.

Marcellus didn't seem to notice. He continued, "We met a few times, Divicia and me. After our first chance encounter."

I didn't let my astonishment show. If Layla hadn't been with us, I would certainly have asked more questions.

They met a few times? A Roman commander and a Celtic noblewoman? What was Marcellus trying to imply? Had he had a love affair with this Divicia? In any case, his report did not make me think of a political exchange.

"After a while we lost track of each other," he continued. "Divicia had spoken about a trip to Gaul that she had to take. Then she disappeared from one day to the next."

"And now she has reappeared, at your palace in the camp?"

I must confess that a glimmer of hope flashed through me. Could this Divicia possibly be a competitor for Layla? And thanks to her, would I get the chance to win back my beloved Nubian?

"It's not a private visit," Marcellus said quickly. "And she can't possibly stay with me at the legate's palace."

"Why not?" I asked, although I thought I already knew the answer. I looked over at Layla, and she gave me a smile that revealed absolutely nothing. Even so, it made me think that she knew everything there was to know about this mysterious Celt.

Layla always seemed to know. During the summer the series of murders had taken place, she had been the one to solve the mystery in the end.

Was Layla against this female acquaintance of her lover's? I was not to know. For Marcellus's next words made me instantly forget any concern for my love life.

He drew breath with a deep sigh and said, "I cannot grant Divicia my hospitality ... because she is a druid."

III

Marcellus's words struck my head like lightning from the gods' heaven.

"A *druid*?" I repeated, dazed.

"Yes, my friend."

"But that's—" This time it was I who struggled to find the right words.

A druid, in the heart of Vindobona, in the legate's palace? This Divicia must be tired of life. And Marcellus, too, apparently, if he had granted her entry into the legionary camp.

The Romans were extremely tolerant in religious matters; they welcomed every new god, no matter how insignificant, into their pantheon. Every citizen of the Empire could indulge in his own personal cult, precisely as he pleased. In Vindobona, people sacrificed not only to the Roman gods, but also to the Celtic, the Germanic, and to numerous others from all corners of the known world. Not even Christianity was officially forbidden—although these extremists refused to honor the gods in the proper way.

Druidism, however, was outlawed on pain of death. The druids instilled panic in the otherwise fearless Romans. Whatever people might say about the Christians, the abominations that circulated about the Celts and their priests far outshone them. The druids were powerful sorcerers and decorated their sacred groves with the severed heads of their enemies. They tortured people to death to sacrifice them to their dark gods, whose thirst for blood seemed unquenchable.

The Emperor Augustus had already forbidden Roman citizens the celebration of druidic rites. Under the reign of Tiberius, a law had been passed against druids, soothsayers, and quacks, and finally Emperor Claudius had done everything humanly possible to eradicate druidism once and for all.

That was now a good eighty years previously. But the druids were persistent, or at least some of them were. Some had become Roman priests, had Romanized their shrines, and now worshipped their old gods under new names. Others, however, had gone underground and continued to operate in secret. They had retreated to the borders of the known world, to the outermost fringes of Gaul or to Britain. But they still lived and worked in the midst of us, in secret sanctuaries hidden deep in the woods, and thus eluded even the long arm of Roman law. At least, that is what was whispered behind closed doors.

Of course, you couldn't tell by looking at a Celtic noblewoman that she was also a druid. But this Divicia had to be foolhardy—no, practically suicidal!—to have visited Marcellus in the legionary camp of Vindobona, whether she were his mistress or not. If it leaked out that she belonged to the druidic priesthood, the legate had to expect serious trouble. Even a man in his position was not invulnerable.

"Divicia has come to Vindobona to offer me something," Marcellus said, snapping me out of my thoughts. "Something that has the potential to change the world, if she tells the truth. And in the process, she could also advance my career and my family's reputation," he added, without mincing words.

Marcellus knew how to arouse my curiosity. No, he was really putting me on the rack with his mysterious hints.

"Perhaps she has heard of Iulius Paulus," he continued, "of the deeds he performs in the name of his god. In any case, she claims her gods have given her a magic that dwarfs all the miracles of the Christians! "

I could no longer hold on to myself. "Now tell me, Marcellus! What did she offer you?"

Marcellus smiled patronizingly. He clearly was enjoying torturing me. And he was no doubt proud that this Divicia had turned to him of all people, regardless of the danger she was putting him in.

Now, finally, he let the cat out of the bag: "Divicia claims that her gods have given her a medicine that can cure the plague."

For a moment there was dead silence in my dining room. At first I thought I had misheard, but that was not the case. Horrified, I jumped up from my sofa. "The Black Death?" I croaked, stricken with a sudden hoarseness.

Marcellus confirmed it with a nod of his head. The smile that played around the corners of his mouth turned into an expression of triumph.

Layla examined me with her eyes narrowed to dark slits. She surely had known long ago what her lover had just revealed to me. She was not a woman from whom any secret could be kept. At any rate, I had never succeeded in doing so, and I doubted whether Marcellus fared any better in this regard.

"Do you understand the implications?" Marcellus asked me. "If Divicia speaks the truth...."

"But how could she?" I interjected. "A cure for the plague? How could there be such a thing?"

A man struck by the sun god Apollo's plague arrows was doomed to death, in ninety-nine of one hundred cases. Hardly anyone survived this worst of all divine plagues.

"Well, I can't imagine why the immortals would want to demonstrate their power to us in Vindobona of all places," said Marcellus, "but apparently we have not attracted the attention of this Christian god only. The gods of the Celts would also like to have us on their side. Divicia, after all, demands a high price for her magic remedy."

"A price?"

"A quid pro quo, if you will. She demands that the ban placed on druidism in the Empire be lifted. She wants to give us her medicine in exchange for the emperor's permission to practice her cult freely again, without persecution, and throughout the Empire."

An exclamation of pure astonishment escaped my throat. What audacity! This Divicia must really be an extraordinary woman. Or raving mad. "And you're supposed to intercede for her with the emperor?" I concluded.

Marcellus nodded. Apparently, his self-confidence was great enough for that. He did not seem to be worried whether and even how he should obtain a personal audience with the Emperor Hadrianus.

"I have already consulted the oracles on how to proceed with Divicia's offer," he continued. "But the results were contradictory. As is often the case, the gods shroud themselves in ambiguity. So I decided to put Divicia and her miracle medicine to the test."

I didn't understand what he meant at first. Sometimes I can be quite slow on the uptake.

"Marcellus wants to take Divicia to a place where the plague is raging right now," Layla explained to me, definitely noticing my confusion.

"That's right," the legate confirmed. "But for such a journey everything needs to be well prepared in advance," he added. "I will be indispensable in Vindobona for another six or seven days, but after that we can leave. And I want to use the time until then to send messengers to neighboring legionary camps. The plague is always raging somewhere. We just need to find out where it is at the moment."

"I will accompany you on this journey," I offered spontaneously. I don't know what possessed me to make this suggestion; I guess I thought that I understood, now, why Marcellus had come to my house with this story about the druid and her medicine. What he wanted to ask of me. He could not well make this journey accompanied by his legionaries; no one was to know that he was traveling with a druidess, at least not before her alleged cure had proven its effectiveness.

"I know my way around," I added, "in the near and far vicinity of Vindobona. And some of my men can give us escort."

To ensure the safety of my trade transports, a good dozen strong and battle-hardened men were at my service at all times.

Marcellus was silent for a moment. He was probably

thinking about what he was risking in carrying out this plan. He was not only putting his career in jeopardy, but his life also, if he voluntarily traveled to a plague-ridden region. But in any case he was apparently prepared to do so.

"I'd like to come, too," I heard Layla say. "I want to learn from Divicia. I've only known her for a short time, but she seems like a truly wise woman. I want to take advantage of the time she is with us. And I want to travel as well, to finally see something of the world!"

"See something of the world?" I snapped. "I'm certainly not going to take you to a place where the Black Death is currently raging!" For a moment I'd forgotten that I was no longer Layla's master, that she was now a freedwoman who could decide for herself where she went.

She had already asked me several times to take her along on smaller trading trips, since I had set her free, and I'd taken her on short journeys in recent months, much to Marcellus's displeasure. To Carnuntum and up the Danubius, to Lentia, Ovilava and to Lauriacum, and it seemed Layla wanted more.

But a journey to an area of disease? Marcellus was protesting even more vehemently than I had. "That's far too dangerous," he cried with fervor. "Out of the question!"

But I knew Layla well. In the end, she would get her way. She had the gift of wrapping both Marcellus and me around her finger as she pleased. In the end, we both always gave in to her wishes, no matter how outlandish or even crazy they might be. I don't know how she did it; her magic powers did not seem to be much inferior to those of the druids.

Marcellus turned back to me. "Thank you for your offer,

Thanar," he said, "I will be glad if you will join me on this journey."

He was silent for a moment. "But what I really wanted to ask you, my friend ... would you grant Divicia and her entourage hospitality under your roof? Just for a few days, until we can leave. I've taken them in for the time being at my palace, but they can't stay there. I'm sure you understand—sooner or later something would leak out. Sooner rather than later; you know how gossipy slaves and servants can be. And legionaries."

I was really slow on the uptake. So this was the reason why Marcellus had come to me; he was not at all concerned with the journey that was about to take place.

"I understand," I said slowly and with more bitterness than I had intended. "If you place your druidic guest with your barbarian friend out of town, the citizens of Vindobona will be more understanding."

"Come on, Thanar," Marcellus replied. "No one will know that she is a druid. No one will even know you are hosting a guest. You are not the center of attention as I am."

This was not flattering either, but undoubtedly Marcellus was right in his assertion.

"And you have good men who can provide for Divicia's safety," he added quickly. "I will arrange for the patrols on the Danubius's shores to be reinforced. But I think Divicia will be in no danger as long as no one learns of her mission."

"I could take care of her, Thanar, if you shelter her under your roof," Layla interjected. "She will want for nothing, and you would not be inconvenienced by her presence."

I tried not to let it show, but Layla had once again managed to change my mind with just a few words. The prospect of having her near me for a few days would probably have me even give Iulius Paulus and his strange god my hospitality! And—I must admit—I was also a little curious about this mysterious Divicia, who had so managed to win Layla over. I wanted to meet her, this druidess who claimed to be able to cure the incurable, and who was trying to negotiate a pact with the Roman emperor himself.

So it was no surprise that I gave my consent to Marcellus—unaware of the deadly adventure on which I was embarking.

IV

The very next afternoon, I awaited the arrival of the Celt and her entourage.

My estate was bustling with activity. Everywhere servants were sweeping and mopping; in the kitchen preparations were underway to feed the expected guests appropriately, and I myself stood in the atrium of my house, looking up to the sky. Dark clouds were gathering above my head, and an icy storm wind was blowing around my ears. I pulled my fur tighter around my freezing limbs.

The signs that the inhabitants of Vindobona had angered the gods could no longer be denied. The never-ending storms that had plagued us in the fall and that had destroyed half of the harvest had been followed by an early, merciless onset of winter. Wolves and bears were coming out of the woods and invading settlements and homesteads. They snatched horses, goats and sheep—the sad remnants of live-stock that had not already frozen to death. And countless houses in Vindobona had fallen victim to a conflagration or some other misfortune in the last few months.

Only a few days ago, I had visited the camp suburb—and almost couldn't recognize it. An eerie silence had spread through the streets; only the wind whistled; hardly a living person was to be seen. Many of the simple wooden houses and hovels of the poor had already been destroyed by the storms, and even the beggars and the homeless, the poorest of the poor, had crawled into holes in the ground, because otherwise they would inevitably have frozen to death.

Hard-frozen animal carcasses lay next to the streets. At least the icy cold was sparing the passers-by the bestial stench of decay.

The voices were growing louder that it was Iulius Paulus, the apostle of this strange Christian god, who had invoked the wrath of the immortals on Vindobona. It was the punishment of the gods for the fact that he and the growing number of his followers refused to sacrifice and pray in the temples.

And now a druidess had showed up in our town, who claimed to possess a remedy against the Black Death.

Was the apocalypse, the end of the world, really upon us, as Paulus preached? The end of the world was one of his absolute favorite topics. "The Day of Judgment is near, Thanar!" he had proclaimed to me whenever I'd crossed his path in recent weeks. "The end of all time, when God will descend to earth to judge humanity. Repent and profess the true faith before it is too late!"

According to Paulus, Christians had been expecting the apocalypse ever since their leader was crucified. That is, for a good hundred years. But Paulus was nevertheless certain that the end of days was imminent now, of all times. The signs were clear, he claimed.

My thoughts returned to Divicia, to the most heinous of evils that she was supposedly able to defeat.

The Black Death. These words awakened the worst memories of my life. I had already met the plague face to face; it had stolen my wife from me. And even though that had been ages ago, not a day went by when I didn't think of my beloved Iduna and miss her sorely.

A gust of wind, which almost swept me off my feet, brought me back from my dark memories to the present. If even here, within the protective walls of my atrium, the storm could develop such power, how might it be raging outside?

Would Marcellus even be able to get as far as my house with my Celtic guests? The distance from the legion's camp was less than two miles, but even such a short journey could become a struggle for survival if one got caught in a storm. Would the north wind sweep the riders from their saddles? Would the bridge that spanned the Danubius withstand the wrath of the gods?

It was not until dusk that the clatter of hooves was finally heard outside the gate. I myself was there to receive the arrivals, even before the slave who was on duty at the gate.

Layla fell around my neck in greeting, which warmed my heart more than any flames in the fireplace might have.

Marcellus was not accompanied by his usual retinue of soldiers. He did not even get out of the saddle, but returned directly to the legionary camp. He mumbled something about urgent matters waiting for him there, and then he was gone.

Divicia, the druidess, rode in the company of two Celtic warriors and a beautiful young woman who, like herself, was wrapped in flowing robes. One of her adepts, I guessed; pupil and assistant at the same time. It was said that young aspirants had to study and practice in the retinue of an experienced druid for up to twenty years before they were allowed to claim this honorable title themselves.

Divicia slid out of the saddle of her stately horse like a skilled rider, and strode toward me like a queen. The wind and the cold seemed to have no effect on her. Wasn't it said that the druids could even impose their will on the elements?

Quickly, I instructed my slaves to care for my guests' mounts and escorted Layla, Divicia and the others into my house. I had warm wine ready for them, spoke the traditional greetings of my people, and welcomed them into my home.

Divicia put on a smile that seemed almost as mysterious as the one Layla so often enchanted me with, and thanked me warmly for my hospitality.

She had an impressive appearance, just as I had imagined her. Even though she was certainly not yet thirty years old, her hair fell in snow-white strands down to her hips. Perhaps she had already seen too much in her visions, had come too close to the realm of the gods, and so was suffering premature signs of old age. In the same way, some prophetesses and oracles might have lost their eyesight during their sacred duty.

Around Divicia's neck was a magnificent torc of gold—one of those necklaces with which the Celtic nobility loved to adorn themselves. More than any other people, the Celts had a passion for the noblest of metals. They hoarded gold in their temples, sank it in lakes and ponds to the glory of their gods, and wore it for display in the form of the magnificent jewelry created by their artisan smiths.

Divicia's adept, whose name was Morann, also wore her

hair down. Both women seemed to think nothing of the complicated hairstyles that were so popular among the Romans. Morann was a beautiful young woman, but so small and delicately built that there was something childlike about her.

The two warriors who accompanied the women, on the other hand, towered a good hand's breadth above even me, and I am truly no dwarf. They too wore golden torcs, and under their cloaks flashed elaborately crafted swords of the best Celtic steel.

The steel of the Celts is famous, and sought after throughout the Empire. Even the Roman legions liked to use it for their weapons.

These two men, who called themselves Granis and Cobanix, were not simple guards of low status. Their clothing, demeanor, and choice of words made it clear that they themselves belonged to the nobility. A truly classy escort; Divicia was surely held in the highest esteem. And the two warriors must have been twin brothers, for they looked so much alike that one could hardly tell them apart.

I gave the women two of my most comfortable guest rooms, and put the twin warriors in the room right next to them. Surely Divicia and Morann would feel safest knowing their companions were close by. Although, at this point, I could have sworn that the security of my house was quite excellent. What a gross miscalculation.

Not only had I made my home more beautiful and comfortable in recent months, but I had also taken advantage of the unusually dry summer to do extensive expansion work. Secretly, I knew why I was doing this: to distract myself from the fact that I had lost Layla to Marcellus.

After the death of my wife many years ago, I had thrown myself into work. I had taken business trips year in and year out, sparing no risk to myself. At that time, I had laid the foundation for my current wealth and status. But now, two decades later, my heart was as empty as it had been during that darkest period of my life.

This time, however, I felt little desire for trade journeys. My servants were taking care of those now, at least when it came to the longer, more arduous traveling. So I had thrown myself into the beautification of my home.

Well, at least I could offer the Celtic nobles an accommodation that they would find appealing. Originally, I had built my house in the style of my ancestors. It had once been a small Germanic homestead, but now I had almost completely transformed it into a luxurious Roman country villa. Only a few rooms were still reminiscent of my barbarian heritage, as Marcellus liked to joke.

For Layla, as always, I kept her usual room ready, located right next to mine. In summer it offered a wonderful view over the Danubius, and as far as the furnishings were concerned, it was by now probably the most beautiful room in the whole house. Besides the new bed with its graceful ivory carvings, Layla had a spacious dressing chest with silver fittings at her disposal. Next to the exit that led to the terrace in summer, I had placed a bronze statue of the divine Mercury.

Layla must want for nothing when she was with me. Although of course I knew that my house could not compete with the legate's palace that Marcellus had recently occupied, no matter how much effort I made, I also knew that while Layla loved beautiful things, her true passion was for something else entirely. For example, my collection of books, which I had gathered in my library from all corners of the Empire. Second, traveling, exploring the world. Third, an occupation that was actually quite unsuitable for women: the investigation of crimes, preferably murder. However, at this point I was hardly thinking about Layla's abilities in this regard.

V

That first evening, I entertained my Celtic guests with a sumptuous dinner, followed by polite chit-chat in the library. Divicia and her entourage were all highly educated and knowledgeable about art. They found great pleasure in my books, and admired the murals, carpets and sculptures.

Layla's dark eyes shone like two stars. It was impossible to miss how much she was enjoying the company of the two women. I had no doubt that they would become best friends within a few days.

Divicia remained deliberately vague about the location of her home, although Layla and I inquired about it several times during the evening meal. As a priestess of a forbidden religion, she probably did not live in one of her people's settlements, but in a secret place known only to initiates.

From some hints she dropped, however, I gathered that her sacred grove must lie two or three days' journey south of Vindobona. She spoke of seven priestesses who lived and studied in this place and celebrated the ancient rites of their faith. They cured the sick, healed the possessed, predicted the future. Layla even told me later that Morann had whispered the most incredible stories about Divicia to her behind closed doors. She was the most powerful druid of her people, Morann claimed. Supposedly, she could even command water and fire, transform into a bear or a wolf, and talk to trees.

"Oh, I wish I could study with Divicia," Layla exclaimed with fervor in between telling me these fantastic stories. I had rarely heard her talk so passionately about anything.

I imagined a sanctuary hidden deep in the forest where Divicia and her followers performed the bloody rites of their faith. The next moment I scolded myself for being a fool. Was the faith of the druids so different from that of my own people? Our tribes also had seers, wise women, and healers. And the Romans also accused us of all kinds of abominations—even human sacrifices.

Divicia was even more cagey about the cure for the plague that the gods had supposedly given her than she was about the location of her home. Layla's curiosity about this medicine was almost a little unbridled, violating the dictates of good hospitality. Nevertheless, the white-haired priestess patiently answered each of her questions with a mysterious smile, and a few words worthy of an oracle. The strangest— and at the same time the most concrete—thing she was willing to tell us about the cure was as follows: "The gods showed me in a vision that the food which we think to be spoiled can develop the most miraculous healing powers."

That made no sense at all, in my opinion. Divicia, however, claimed that she had already been able to achieve miraculous successes with the mysterious medicine within not only her own tribal community, but also within a whole number of friendly Celtic tribes. In nine out of ten cases, she claimed, the plague sufferers she had treated had survived.

This was nothing short of a miracle, because normally it was the other way around. The plague usually killed nine out of ten of its victims. The Black Death regularly depopulated entire villages, not only in the Empire, but also in faraway Asia. At least, that's what I had heard from credible sources.

I could understand that Divicia did not want to reveal her secrets to us; the plague remedy could be her key to a future of freedom. If her medicine were really effective, I knew Marcellus wouldn't hesitate to take it all the way to the supreme ruler. And perhaps the Emperor Hadrianus could be persuaded to lift the ban on druidism by imperial decree.

VI

During the next two days we neither heard nor saw anything of Marcellus. He was probably preoccupied with his urgent business in the legionary camp, which he had to attend to before our departure. And he had also to wait and see from which places in the immediate vicinity his messengers would come to report existing plague outbreaks. I was looking forward to this journey, which would put Divicia and her magic medicine to the test, with very mixed feelings.

The weather was still deteriorating, although that hardly seemed possible. It remained bitterly cold, but now snow was also falling from the sky in thick white flakes, and you could hardly see your own hand in front of your eyes. The storm had seamlessly turned into a blizzard.

If it continued like this, the weather would make our planned journey impossible. Even the messengers that Marcellus had sent out would have a hard time reaching their destinations and returning safely to Vindobona.

Divicia and her entourage, however, were pleasant and very low-maintenance guests. They always behaved politely, showing gratitude for every dish, every cup of wine. Granis and Cobanix, the two warriors, kept to themselves and talked mostly in their own language, which I did not understand. But they also responded with friendly words and in the best manner when spoken to. And they seemed to feel safe in my care. Divicia and Morann moved freely throughout the house, carefree, without the two guards feeling the need to protect them at every step. I liked that; it was important to me to be a good host.

When late at night, on the third day after the arrival of the Celts, there was suddenly a knock on my bedroom door, I jumped out of bed in joyful expectation. I ran to the door expecting to see Layla in front of me, who might possibly not be able to sleep and be pining for me.

However, I encountered one of my guard slaves, who was in a flurry of excitement. "Legate Marcellus desires admittance," the words burst from him even before I had fully opened the door.

"At this time of night? In this weather?" I could hear the storm howling around the house; when I had gone to bed, the snow had already been piled up knee-deep outside the walls.

I followed my slave through the dark corridors. Everybody was already asleep, and nowhere was a light to be seen or the slightest sound to be heard.

"Where is Marcellus?" I asked the lad. "You didn't make him wait outside the gate, I hope? You know he's a special friend of the house—"

My slave cut me off. Which was usually not his style at all, but the excitement apparently had made him forget his good manners. "He's not alone, master. The—" He bit his lips and stopped abruptly, so that I almost ran into him.

"Speak up, man," I said, a little incensed.

"The blasphemers, master! The legate has brought them

with him."

Although I had not yet found sleep, I felt a little dizzy. I did not understand what my slave was talking about, and impatiently left him standing in the hallway, crossed the atrium in a few quick steps, and pushed aside more of my slaves who had gathered around the front gate.

The gate was standing open, the storm blowing snow inside, and the freezing cold was getting into my bones. I had only put on a simple tunic when I'd hurried to the door of my bedroom—in the expectation of getting rid of this garment immediately again, in order to dedicate myself to the joys of love. But this was no longer to be thought of tonight; I grasped that with a glance at the new arrivals.

Marcellus was just pressing the reins of his horse into the hand of one of my lads.

Next to him, a soldier I had seen in Marcellus's entourage before jumped out of the saddle. He was no ordinary legionary, but a centurion named Severus, if I remembered correctly. I estimated him to be in his mid-thirties, even though his angular skull was almost bald. His nose looked as if it had been broken several times.

Then my eyes fell on the carriage that had come to a halt directly behind Marcellus. It was an expensive travel wagon, the kind that only wealthy citizens could afford. The two heavy steeds that were harnessed to it were puffing their guts out. Their bodies steamed in the icy winter air. It must have cost the animals an enormous effort to transport the heavy vehicle over the snow-covered streets to my house.

This car did not belong to the legion, that was immediately clear to me—but I didn't have time for any further speculations. At that moment, I spotted a familiar face in the front window of the vehicle.

VII

I took a step further out into the cold, which I barely noticed now, spellbound with astonishment, and squinted my eyes to see better.

No, I was not mistaken. In that posh wagon that had braved the raging elements in the middle of the night and headed for my house sat Iulius Paulus, the argentarius of Vindobona. Or rather, the apostle of the Christian god. He looked at me gravely and then hurriedly climbed out of the wagon.

Marcellus seemed to be on high alert. He barked at Severus to secure the perimeter of my house, as if expecting an attack at any moment.

Behind the centurion, two legionaries emerged from the blizzard, obeying wordlessly and scanning the environment with wary gazes. They looked as if they were going into battle against the hosts of the underworld. And Severus cast glances at Paulus that left no doubt where he saw the center of danger: in the atheist, to whom he had surely only very reluctantly given escort to my house.

Obedience and fulfillment of duty were the first priority for every Roman soldier. If the legate gave an order to protect a Christian, this order was executed, without contradiction or discussion. But if Severus had had his way, he would have visibly preferred to stone Paulus rather than escort him.

Marcellus looked around in all directions, and didn't seem to want to come inside until the last passenger had climbed out of the travel wagon. He stepped close to me and put a hand on my shoulder. "I know it's a lot to ask, my friend, but could you take on a few more guests?"

He pointed with his hand to Paulus, who was helping two women climb out of the wagon. One of them I recognized as Philomena, Paulus's wife.

In the past, when her husband had been held in the highest esteem by the citizens of Vindobona, she had been the epitome of a Roman matron. She had been a proud woman, who embodied prosperity and modesty, who always dressed in the latest fashion and wore the hairstyle that the emperor's wife in Rome dictated.

Now, however, Philomena looked like a disheveled field mouse fleeing from a bird of prey. She wore an expensive fur cape, but her hair fell in tangled strands into her face, and naked fear for her life could be read in her unmade-up eyes.

I was also familiar with the second woman who was traveling with the couple, and who now also ventured out of the carriage: Caecilia, a freedwoman of Paulus, who had worked in his business for many years and whom I had therefore met many times. She was so devoted to Paulus that some gossipers rumored she was more than just his servant.

Whether there was any truth in that, I didn't care. She was young, a little skinny, but she had beautiful flaxen hair and almost always a friendly smile on her lips. What I knew for sure, however, was that Caecilia had recently become as ardent a follower of Christianity as Paulus himself was.

Finally, a man climbed out of the travel wagon, a giant

whom every child in Vindobona knew. His name was Flamma, and he had once been the most famous gladiator in the province. Now, however, he was considered a follower of Paulus and his god also.

"The situation in Vindobona has escalated," Marcellus explained to me. He was visibly trying to radiate calm and level-headedness, just like the commander whom nothing could shake. But I couldn't help noticing that his voice was trembling.

"I had to get Paulus out of the city," he continued, "otherwise I could no longer have guaranteed his safety. A mob has gathered at the gates of the legionary camp and demanded his head. "

"By all the gods—how did that happen?" I asked.

Marcellus made a snide hand gesture. "Wolves have invaded the town. They have killed some cattle, and an infant—a clear sign that Vindobona has finally forfeited the favor of the gods. This was the last straw; a mob quickly formed, armed with clubs and stones, and moved in front of the Christians' house. If it hadn't been for the fact that Flamma was staying with Paulus for dinner—" Marcellus rolled his eyes dramatically. "They would have massacred him on the spot."

"But then no one dared to mess with Flamma, the legendary swordsman?" I speculated. "Not even an angry mob."

"Still, it didn't take much," Marcellus said. "They smashed the front gate. The servants ran for their lives. Paulus was just able to grab the two women, himself and a few belongings. They fled to the legionary camp with the wagon and pleaded for protection. Flamma remained faithfully at their side."

"And you couldn't take them in, or you would have risked a riot," I ventured.

Marcellus nodded grimly. "Within a short time there were about five hundred people who had gathered in front of the camp gate, loudly demanding the execution of the Christians. *To the lions, to the lions!* they shouted in chorus. *All of them!* Of course, I could have put down this uprising by force, but that would not have solved the problem. Paulus is no longer safe in Vindobona. And the majority of the legionaries also expected a judgment from me. One that restored peace with the gods."

Marcellus frowned. "I had to act; I had no choice. So I proclaimed the banishment of Paulus and his followers, to send them into exile this very night. To emphasize my words, I immediately rode off with them in person. I made the mob believe that I would take the Christians across the Danubius and leave them here to their fate. Which satisfied the plebs' bloodthirstiness for the time being."

VIII

The legate knocked the snow off his cloak and looked around for his men, but they had long since disappeared into the darkness, probably checking the surroundings of my estate. Did they seriously think that someone had followed them all the way from Vindobona? That someone would attack my house?

"Severus is trustworthy," Marcellus said. "So are his legionaries. Even if they—like every other man in the camp—would have preferred to see an execution. They did their best to make sure we made it this far at all. Curse this winter!"

"I'm surprised you're so committed to Paulus," I said.

"Let the lightning strike him for all I care! But I will not tolerate riots in my town. Nor vigilante mob justice!"

"And what is to become of him now?" I asked. "Have you thought about that yet?"

The idea of welcoming these Christians, who had unleashed the wrath of the gods, into my home of all places, filled me with fear and terror. Why deny it? Was that why I was still standing out here in the cold, drilling Marcellus with my questions?

The Christians, however, seemed to have similar reservations. They crowded close together in the lee of their wagon and conferred in excited whispers. Were they deliberating whether to ask for refuge in the house of a pagan? Didn't they realize that they had no other choice in this weather?

I, for one, surrendered to my fate with a sigh. I knew that I could not turn them away, as much as I would have liked to.

"I'm sorry, Thanar," said Marcellus, who seemed to know exactly what was going on inside me. "I didn't see any other way. Paulus will have to go into hiding for a few days. After that, I will see to it that his belongings are packed—what is left of them. Probably at this very moment his house is being already looted. I will see to it that he gets a good price for his estate and can build a new life elsewhere, all without too much fuss."

I nodded. Marcellus had acted thoughtfully in the midst of the crisis, as befitted a good leader.

"But first, he and his followers need a roof over their heads. Just for a few days. I have no choice but to ask for your hospitality once again, Thanar. I hope you won't hold it against me." Marcellus stared somberly at the sky. "Hospitality for all of us, I'm afraid," he added. "I don't think we'll be able to make our way back to camp tonight in this weather."

"You are always welcome to me," I said. "And you know that. But who will you bring me next? First druids, now Christians..."

I left the sentence unfinished and instead tried to put on a brave smile, but I failed. My teeth were chattering. Only now did I realize how miserably I was freezing, even though I hadn't been paying attention.

I invited the Christians into my house—anxious to make my words sound hospitable rather than beset by fear. Paulus thanked me graciously, then he and his party quickly got moving. They had probably come to the conclusion that my roof was their best—no, their only—hope for the night.

I gave orders to my slaves to take care of the wagon and the horses. Two of my servants loaded the few luggage items of the newcomers onto their shoulders, while others helped them make their way to my house through the deep snow. One of my sturdy guard slaves carried Caecilia in his arms, and Flamma did the same for Philomena. He lifted her as if she were a skinny child and not a well-fed Roman matron.

The citizens of Vindobona are actually quite a peace-loving bunch. The fact that they had turned into bloodthirsty beasts, trying to claim the lives of several people, only showed how desperate they must be. The wrath of the gods was feared more than anything else, and not only among the common people. Would I now bring down the vengeance of the immortals on my home if I took in Paulus and the other atheists?

Tacitus wrote about the Germanic tribes that *no other people have such an unlimited passion for hospitality*. Flattering words—but my hospitality was in a very bad way tonight. Fortunately, my house was at least spacious enough to accommodate the newcomers without any problems.

Just as I was about to have the gate locked again, a lone rider appeared in front of my house, emerging out of the darkness like a ghost.

His horse collapsed under him as he dismounted, and the man himself, in the wild rush of the snow, resembled a being from another world. But then, as he dragged himself with his last strength to the gate and thus into the glow of the torches, I recognized him.

"Thessalos!" I shouted in disbelief, and rushed to his aid before he fell. Marcellus reacted just as quickly and jumped to the man's left side.

The completely exhausted rider was one of the physicians of the legionary camp, a young Greek and in my opinion the best medic in Vindobona. He had only recently saved my life.

In the course of the terrible series of murders that had taken place only a few months before, I'd almost fallen victim to an insidious assassination attempt. It was only thanks to the medical skill of this young doctor that I was still on this side of the river of death.

"Are you out of your mind?" Marcellus gruffly addressed the man. "What are you doing here? Why did you follow us?"

"I thought ... you would..." Thessalos gasped, but then words failed him.

Marcellus' youthful features hardened. Angered, he stared at the half-frozen medicus. "You thought I would lead Paulus and the others to their graves? Leave them to the elements, to freeze to death?"

Thessalos nodded wordlessly while we dragged him into the house so that I could finally have the gate locked against the snow and cold.

"You were going to save them, those Christians?" Marcellus asked incredulously. "Don't tell me you ... you're not one of them, are you, Thessalos?"

The Greek struggled for breath. Gratefully, he wrapped himself in a woolen blanket that a servant had quickly brought. "Not that, Legate," he said when he had regained his speech. "But Paulus is a great healer, whatever you may think of his god. He must not be allowed to die! I have seen him cure the possessed at Vindobona, where our healing art failed. How he made the blind see and the lame walk again. He made them recover, with nothing but the power of his faith. I could not allow—"

Marcellus tapped the man on the shoulder, interrupting his sudden torrent of words. "Don't worry, Thessalos. I never intended to abandon the Christians to the elements. As you can see, they are well and safe, here under Thanar's roof. But you must be weary of living to follow our tracks on a night like this!"

With an agonized sigh directed at me, Marcellus added, "May I ask you for another bed for the night, Thanar?"

"Thessalos is always welcome to me," I replied.

The doctor smiled wearily. "Thank you, old friend."

Turning to Marcellus, he continued, "I should not have doubted you, Legate. You are not inhuman. Please forgive me! I should have realized that you would not send the Christians to certain death."

Marcellus nodded benignly.

I led my guests into one of the dining rooms, which was well heated, and instructed my servants to bring warm wine, bread and cheese, and fat sausages, so that the new arrivals could fortify themselves. In the meantime, I went over in my mind who I should best put up where. My house was large, but not a palace with an endless number of rooms.

I decided to put Thessalos the doctor, and Severus the centurion, together in one of the remaining guest rooms, and I would have the two legionaries stay in the servants' quarters. Ordinary soldiers are not at all spoiled when it comes to accommodation. In the legionary camp, they share narrow quarters, with bunk beds and a cooking area, in groups of eight or ten.

This left a spacious room for Paulus and his wife, as well as an additional room that the Christians asked me for, as if from one mouth. They wanted to gather there for common prayers and to pay homage to their god.

Flamma and Caecilia were then left with two smaller chambers, but they each occupied them with words of gratitude—addressed to me and to their god, who had led them to a safe shelter in their hour of greatest need, as Caecilia put it.

"The Lord led us to the safe stable, like he did with Joseph and Mary," Paulus added unctuously.

I didn't find it very flattering that he compared my house to a stable, but what did I understand about the strange ideas of these Christians?

Paulus decorated the prayer room I provided for them with a cross, a chalice and a bowl from his travel chest. Apparently, these were utensils that played an important role in the rituals of his cult.

All four Christians soon retreated to this room, and soft murmurs of voices and chants could still be heard through the walls when I was already heading for my bedroom.

Finally, I assigned Marcellus to a chamber that was certainly worthy of a legate, but at the maximum possible distance from Layla's room. That was probably foolish of me, since the two of them spent the majority of their nights together—but I didn't want to have to imagine them as lovers under my own roof.

The few hours until dawn passed without any special incidents. It was the proverbial calm before the storm, before the catastrophe came upon us.

IX

There is hardly a group of people among whom news—especially those that one would actually like to keep secret—spreads faster than among house servants.

When Divicia and her entourage had arrived, I had not mentioned to my servants with a word that she was a druid priestess. Nevertheless, only a few hours later the whispers began, and I am sure that the following day even the least of my servants was aware of whom I had accepted as a guest in my house.

The argentarius and his followers were infamous anyway, of course. Everyone in Vindobona knew that Iulius Paulus had recently become an apostle of the Lord, as he liked to put it. And what was known in Vindobona had made its way within a very short time to my house also. My servants and slaves regularly frequented the town. When they visited the market, a tavern, the temples in the forum or the amphitheater, they gossiped passionately with the servants of other families. Thus, in most cases, they were far better informed than I could ever be.

When I introduced Paulus and his people to Divicia and hers on the morning after their arrival, I'd limited myself to introducing them by name. With no word had I mentioned the respective cults to which they adhered. And yet, thanks to my talkative slaves, a few hours later everyone knew who they were dealing with.

As I had expected, this realization was not received with joy in either the druidic or Christian camps. Especially Divicia and Paulus met each other with a coldness and brusqueness, against which the snowstorm still raging around my house suddenly seemed almost homely.

At breakfast, they'd eyed each other skeptically—probably not yet fully aware of who they were dealing with. At lunch, I caught some of the glances they gave each other and felt reminded of lethally sharpened daggers.

Nevertheless there was no open conflict; everyone involved knew how to behave as a guest in a foreign house, for which I thanked the gods.

When it finally came to a fight, to my surprise it was the Christians who got into it. Specifically, in the afternoon I became an involuntary witness to a heated argument between Paulus, his wife Philomena, and Caecilia the freedwoman.

I couldn't hear what they were arguing about, I just saw them standing together gesticulating violently under the arcades of one of the walkways surrounding the courtyards of my house.

I was amazed that they had been drawn outdoors in this weather. Even though the roof of the arcades protected them, the snow in the courtyard was now chest-high, and the wind was gusting right into the very last corners of the walls. Perhaps the Christians had merely retreated here in order to discuss something undisturbed? Due to the large number of guests, my house was bustling with activity all day long.

Of course, I didn't want to eavesdrop, I was just struck by the vehemence of the argument. Philomena seemed indignant at first, but apparently Paulus quickly managed to get her on his side. Caecilia, on the other hand, seemed downright beside herself. She spoke to her former master with a fierceness that was by no means common among freed slaves.

I wondered, but went my way as quickly as possible and soon forgot the incident, for something even stranger claimed my attention only a little while later.

As the afternoon progressed, Paulus and Divicia seemed to suddenly take a liking to each other. I spotted the two of them in the atrium speaking together, smiling politely, and later I encountered them again, this time in the library, where they were still talking. They seemed like old friends who had so much to exchange that their tongues could hardly stop.

Marcellus and his men did not even attempt to make their way back to the legionary camp. On the one hand, the persistent snowstorm made even such a short journey an expedition into the unknown, and might possibly lead to their deaths. Did the gods want to bury Vindobona under the white mass, as the beautiful city of Pompeii had been entombed under the ashes of Vesuvius?

On the other hand, Marcellus was visibly plagued by a guilty conscience for how much he had strained my hospitality by accommodating the atheists with me. Even more so, since I was already hosting his druidess. It must have been clear to him that we were not only provoking the wrath of the gods, but that allowing the two cults to meet in such close quarters was certainly not a recipe for hospitable coexistence. And so Marcellus postponed his return to the legate's palace probably also to stand by me in case the situation escalated.

To my delight, in the morning Marcellus had stepped out of the room I had assigned him, while Layla, for her part, left her bedchamber next to mine. At least there didn't seem to have been a night of love between the two of them under my roof. A consolation, after all.

At dinner, the friendly dialogue between Paulus and Divicia continued. In particular, Paulus treated the druid priestess with exquisite courtesy and praised her wisdom and erudition before all present.

What had happened? How had the two of them been able to overcome their aversion to each other's cult so quickly? I didn't know, and I wasn't supposed to know. I merely picked up a few snippets of their conversation.

Apparently, the dialogue revolved around the persecution of their respective cults. They discussed the rumors, nay, from their point of view, the terrible calumnies that circulated about both the druids and the Christians. Perhaps their sympathy, so suddenly won for each other, was based on nothing more than shared suffering?

In the triclinium, my Roman dining room, it was comfortably warm. Outside, the snow fell relentlessly. In the surrounding forests, the wolves howled.

I had to think of the much-lamented child who had fallen victim to these hungry creatures, in the middle of Vindobona. Was it really the gods who had incited these beasts against us humans?

After dinner, Marcellus confided in me that Paulus had asked him for a talk that afternoon. "Paulus and his entourage want to accompany us," he explained to me. "On our journey toward the Black Death."

Marcellus not only liked to choose dramatic words, he also knew how to give them the necessary effect in a sonorous tone. "Paulus wants to prove to us that his god is also able to heal plague sufferers. Much better than the pagan demons of Divicia, as he put it."

I shook my head in disbelief. "Is he so tired of life, then?" I asked. "And he wants to take the two women with him as well?"

Marcellus nodded. "They even insisted on it themselves. Caecilia, at any rate, announced to me in passionate speech that she did not fear death. And Flamma immediately joined in. If it is their god's will, they are ready to go to their deaths, like a number of their brothers and sisters in the faith before them. Martyrdom, have you heard of it? You could almost think it would be their highest happiness to die like their god, in the most shameful and painful way possible."

"I've read about it," I said, "that some Christians would rather choose death on the cross or in the arena than sacrifice to the gods."

Marcellus hunched his shoulders. "Would you die for Mercury or Jupiter, or whatever your people call them, Thanar?"

I shook my head.

"Neither would I. But I think you don't have to understand these Christians. In any case, I have given Paulus my approval. If we all start the journey together, the question of what is to become of him and his own is solved, at least for the time being. And if his god really proves to be so powerful that he can conquer the plague—well, I then want to be his intercessor, too, just as for Divicia. Then Paulus will possibly be accepted back in Vindobona as well. A delicate situation that requires some tact—"

"But you possess that in abundance," I said with a smile, putting a hand on my friend's shoulder.

I can't say that I was looking forward to the journey towards the Black Death—but on the other hand, I felt a certain curiosity as to what demonstrations of divine power awaited us there.

I didn't get to see Layla all day. It was not until late in the evening that I found her in the library, where she was resting on a couch with a small tome in codex format. She was so engrossed in her reading that she didn't notice me until I leaned over her and placed a kiss on the top of her head.

"What are you reading?" I asked her.

Layla closed the book and handed it to me. "Caecilia lent it to me," she said. "It contains some important writings of her faith. About Jesus' life and what he did."

"So?" I asked, in a deliberately innocuous tone, "What do you think of the Christians? Do you find them as fascinating as our druid priestesses?"

"Caecilia is nice," she said, "a freedwoman like me. She also likes to live in the familia of her former master."

She gave me a smile that warmed my heart. "And this Jesus—their god, or the son of their god, or both at once, it's a little confusing—I find him interesting too. He put up with

57

the least of people, slaves, lepers, prostitutes. He even suffered a criminal's death on the cross himself."

"Don't you find it strange that he—or his divine father—allowed this to happen, when they are such powerful gods?" I interjected. "That he was crucified?"

"Caecilia says he took death upon himself to redeem people from their guilt."

"What guilt?"

"I didn't really understand that either. I think she means that we are under the influence of evil, and that her god wanted to free us from it through his death. But it only works if we believe in him and renounce all other gods." Layla fell silent and looked at me thoughtfully.

"What if this god of the Christians is really a demon?" I said. "Who wants to divide us from the true gods? Doesn't it look like that to you?"

"Hmm," said Layla, then seemed to have had enough of philosophizing for the moment. "Have you noticed that Flamma and Morann have become friends?" she asked me. "Within a single day and despite the cults they adhere to being so different? Isn't that remarkable?"

"Become friends? Are you serious?" The Christian ex-gladiator and the druidic adept? Could one imagine a more mismatched pair than those two?

Flamma had been quite a favorite of women in the days when he'd still thrilled the crowds in the arena, like so many other famous gladiators. In recent months, however, he had been seen only in the company of Paulus and other Christians. He had kept his gladiator name, but Flamma now burned not for a good fight, but exclusively for his god.

And that this man, of all people, should make friends with a druidess—he surely had to regard her as a deluded pagan, if not as a corrupted sorceress!

Layla shrugged as if she had read my mind. "Anyway, the two of them spent the whole day together. I ran into them several times, and they were clearly looking for a quiet spot. And they seemed to enjoy each other's company very much."

"I think that's good, don't you?" I remarked. "Paulus and Divicia also seem to have overcome their initial hostility, after all. Did you notice how animatedly they talked at dinner? It's like they were the best of friends."

Layla smiled and nodded. "It will all come to a good end," she said, "for the druids, for the Christians, and for all of us in Vindobona. Now we just have to defeat the plague. "

X

While the storm that was raging around my house was still growing in strength and rattling the roof beams with angry howls, my guests withdrew one by one for their night's rest.

Only Paulus and Divicia continued their conversation. For this purpose, they went to Divicia's chamber, a beautiful, spacious room with a small table and two chairs. I sent a slave to the cellar to serve them both a select amphora of Falernian wine.

I myself had probably drunk one cup too many at dinner, or mixed too little water with my wine. I was suddenly plagued by a strange dizziness, and my tongue stuck drily to the roof of my mouth.

Marcellus seemed to feel similarly uncomfortable. He withdrew to his room very early with curt words. To my displeasure, he grabbed Layla's hand, kissed her on the neck in front of me, and took her with him. Usually he was much more reserved in expressing his feelings for Layla, at least in my presence.

I decided to go to sleep as well. My dizziness had increased, and now to make matters worse I was sinking into self-pity. I was a lonely old man, deprived of all the pleasures of life. Marcellus was a good friend to me, sometimes almost like the son the gods had never given me. But occasionally I also wished he had never set foot in my house. Then it would have been my turn to lead Layla into my bedroom. And to kiss her neck.

The corridors of my house were already dark and deserted, but I found my way blindly. Was it my imagination, or were the horses outside in the stables in a frenzy? It almost sounded as if they were screaming, not just neighing.

Well, perhaps the continuous whistling and howling of the blizzard was getting to them, in addition to the icy cold, against which even the solidly built stable walls could not protect them, and the howling of the wolves, which had started again. It was a terrible night. And it would become worse still.

I don't know how many hours I slept. When I suddenly woke from a dream, my head felt as if I'd had three full days of feasting with too much wine and overabundant food. My bedstead seemed to sway beneath me, as if I were on board a ship, and the walls surrounding me also curved strangely under my sleep-drunk gaze.

The next moment, I heard myself scream. At the foot of my couch—someone was standing there!

It was a slender, delicate figure with long hair that fell over her shoulders like spun threads of gold. I would have recognized her among thousands: my wife Iduna.

But she is dead, I admonished myself as I staggered out of bed. Carried off by the Black Death!

It had to be a mirage, a chimera from the realm of dreams in which I had just dwelled, or perhaps even still lingered? I rubbed my eyes. No, I was awake—and yet my beloved wife stood before me, in all the beauty and grace she had possessed during her lifetime.

She began to speak before I reached her. "Hear me, Thanar!" Her tone was so serious, almost commanding, that I stumbled and sank back onto my bed. I just sat there, barely able to hold myself upright, staring at her as if paralyzed.

The ground was swaying even more violently under my feet now, and my insides seemed to spin in circles, faster and faster.

"You are not real," I whispered, but Iduna ignored this objection. Her eyes, as dark a green as the endless forests of the north, studied me as if they could see to the bottom of my soul. How much had I loved her—yes, still loved her, even though Layla had now taken the central place in my heart.

The words Iduna spoke did not make the slightest sense, although I heard them clearly. It felt as if they found their way into my head without having to first take the usual detour through my ears.

"Do everything you can to win back Layla's heart," Iduna said. "She belongs to you. She loves you as I once loved you, even though she may not have fully realized it yet. Don't wait until it's too late!"

With these words Iduna, or rather her mirage, disappeared. Darkness and silence spread through the room, and my heart went cold. I must have imagined this encounter. Especially the words! Iduna, advising me to win Layla back? Was this how she was going to make me find new happiness from the realm of the dead? Iduna was the kind of person who always put the welfare of others before her own.

Especially my own well-being. But this was definitely going too far!

What was it that I had heard and seen? I was a rational man, with a clear mind. I was not inclined to delusions!

XI

Shortly thereafter, I fell into a restless sleep. I woke up several times, imagining that I heard voices—but the place at the foot of my bed remained empty. Iduna did not return.

Some philosophers claim that in our dreams the gods speak to us. Or even that our souls ascend to the immortal plane. I couldn't have said where my soul strayed that night, but it certainly wasn't to the heaven of the gods.

Suddenly there was a scream that pierced the darkness. The voice of a woman, half mad with fear. In the next moment, this cry of horror turned into a howl and wail that sounded no less terrifying.

I was certainly not imagining it, I could have sworn to that. I jumped out of bed, staggered, felt for my tunic, which I found at the head of my couch, slipped it on, then had to pause for a moment.

I clung to the frame of the couch to keep myself upright. I was still seized by the same hideous dizziness.

Pull yourself together, I ordered myself, and then my feet finally obeyed me, albeit rather shakily. Mustering all my strength, I staggered out of the room.

In the darkness of the corridors, slaves scurried past me. I heard their voices, saw the occasional flicker of a lamp, but I paid no attention to them. I followed the wailing that still continued—and finally found myself in front of the chamber that I had assigned to Divicia, the druidess.

A few slaves had already gathered in the open doorway, apparently not daring to enter the room, but nevertheless craning their necks curiously. They scattered when they saw me.

I stepped—no, I staggered—into the room and finally almost lost control of my legs.

Quickly a slave was at my side, supporting me.

"I'm all right," I moaned, and vigorously shook him off.

But what I saw in front of me couldn't possibly be real, could it? It had to be another mirage, a delusion, like the appearance of my wife—only infinitely more horrible.

It was dark in the room, with only a single oil lamp flickering on a small table. And yet I saw blood and ruin wherever I turned.

On the couch to my right, I recognized Divicia's figure, stretched out lifeless, bloodied like a sacrificial animal on an altar. Her eyes stared into space, cold and empty like two ice crystals.

She was dead, there could be no doubt about that. Morann was kneeling beside her, holding her hand, muttering stammered words in her language that I didn't understand. Behind her crouched Granis and Cobanix, the two Celtic warriors. Like two bronze statues they knelt there, motionless, wordless.... Only their eyes were staring at Divicia's murdered body, as if they were already holding a wake for their former mistress.

But that was not all. As if in a horrible demonic mirror, I saw an almost identical image of horror to my left. Flamma was standing there. He was supporting Caecilia, who was sobbing uncontrollably. On the floor, right next to them,

Philomena was kneeling—bent deeply over the corpse of her husband.

Iulius Paulus offered the exact mirror image of Divicia, lying lifeless on the floor, his robe stained all over with blood.

I realized that it must have been Philomena whose cries had roused me from my sleep. She was howling and wailing over the lifeless form of her husband, tearing at her hair as if this were the only way she could give vent to the pain in her heart.

Flamma was fortunately able to give me a halfway comprehensible account of events. In any case, he made the attempt. While he continued to hold Caecilia tightly in his arms, he turned to me and began to speak haltingly.

I must confess that I could hardly follow his words. I simply could not comprehend what I was seeing before me.

While the gladiator was talking to me, and I realized that the bloodbath before my eyes was not a mirage, a thought came into my head: *So this is it, the end of the world.* The apocalypse, the Last Judgment, with which Paulus had so gladly threatened the unbelievers. Only it was the apostle himself whom the gods had struck down. Together with Divicia? That made no sense at all!

"We gathered in the prayer room," Flamma said, clearly trying to give me a calm and sober report. His eyes, however, were so dilated that they threatened to pop out of their sockets. "Philomena, Caecilia and I ... we had been haunted by strange visions since nightfall. That's why we came together, to stop the forces of darkness through pious prayer. When it was late, we decided to go to sleep. Philomena went to check on Paulus. We knew he was here with the druidess—

"

With a hateful look, Flamma stared over at the Celts gathered around the dead Divicia. "Paulus had sought dialogue with her, he wanted to speak to her of the Lord … to save her soul. To make her see the error of her ways and lead her to the true faith."

I exhaled deeply and struggled to clear my head. What I saw before me here—what had happened under my roof!—this was no divine judgment. Paulus and Divicia must have died at the hands of men. Someone had stabbed my two guests!

I don't know which notion was more terrifying: the end of the world or two murders under my roof. Yet again! It was barely a few months ago that—

No, now was not the time to think back to those earlier atrocities. That case was closed, over and done with, the murderer judged, the victims avenged.

But this … I forced myself to look more closely at the dead. I blinked first at Divicia, then at Paulus, at their bloodied corpses. The light was dim, but I was reluctant to call for a slave with a torch. The sight was horrific enough in the semi-darkness.

Divicia's pristine white arms were covered with gaping cuts, and on Paulus's strong, hairy limbs I could make out similar marks of a struggle. Someone must have attacked the two of them with a sword or dagger. And this person had succeeded in killing both of his victims. Unnoticed by all the inhabitants of the house!

Why on earth had the attacker felt such a deadly hatred for these two people? Divicia and Paulus had been able to defend themselves with nothing but their bare arms to ward off the knife or sword thrusts of their attacker, and thereby had only managed to delay their deaths.

XII

I let my gaze wander around the room, but there was no trace of the weapon the killer had used.

For the moment I could not take a closer look at the two corpses, because the circle of their respective followers had tightened now around both of them. It was almost as if the survivors wanted to make an attempt—much too late—to save Paulus and Divicia from their cruel fate. But there was nothing left for them to do but weep and lament, and—as for Flamma—to swear with clenched fist deadly revenge on the one who had committed this bloody deed.

Granis and Cobanix immediately threatened Divicia's murderer with an even worse fate.

"It must have been the same man who murdered them both," Granis added, flushed with anger. "Two unarmed people who could not defend themselves. What a cowardly beast!"

Suddenly I felt a warm hand on my arm and heard a familiar voice. "Look, over there in the coal basin," she whispered.

Layla. I knew it was her even before I turned. She looked at me from greatly dilated eyes, framed by dark shadows. She seemed agitated, but not panicked.

My gaze followed her outstretched index finger, which pointed to the brazier. Only a faint glow was still visible there. I didn't understand what Layla found so interesting about it—in a room where two bodies lay!

"The shards," she whispered to me, "don't you see them? Someone has broken an expensive glass vial."

With a few steps, she crossed the room, toward the small heating stove, and pulled me behind her. She pointed to a large, ring-shaped shard of glass stuck between the pieces of coal. "Here, this was the neck of the jar, closed with a wooden plug and originally sealed with wax. The wax lique-fied here at the edge of the basin from the heat of the em-bers."

She knelt down, ran her fingertips over the floor just below the basin, and then showed me remnants of a whitish pow-der that had stuck to her skin.

"And so what?" I said. Didn't we have more worries right now than some broken vessel—even if it might once have been precious?

"Divicia showed it to me when it was still intact. I asked her to let me look at her magic medicine at least once, if she wouldn't tell me anything more about it—and she showed me this vial."

Layla rose again and stared into the shard-strewn embers. "Someone destroyed it," she said, "and it certainly wasn't un-intentional." Her voice sounded changed, as if she were speaking from far away. She spoke more slowly, more pon-derously, than usual.

"Where is the legate?" Granis shouted at me at that mo-ment. "He bears responsibility for these murders. He swore to us Divicia would be safe in your house!" Accusingly, he pointed with his outstretched hand to the lifeless form of the druidess.

Marcellus was not among us. Had he simply slept through

the commotion that must have been heard in the far corners of my house? And that, although Layla had slipped out of his room? She had spent the night with him, as far as I knew.

Layla was a very light sleeper. The slightest movement, the softest sound could wake her up. That was what I remembered from our countless nights together.

I signaled to one of the slaves still crowding in the doorway to wake Marcellus and bring him to us. Eager to serve, he scurried away.

Of course, I did not share the Celtic warrior's opinion that Marcellus bore any responsibility for the horrible bloodshed. I myself could have sworn that both the Celts and the Christians under my roof were as safe as one could be.

I had been wrong. And very much so.

In the next instant, the situation threatened to escalate. Severus, the centurion, appeared in the doorway, followed by his legionaries, who rallied around him as if all their lives were in danger.

Using his hands and elbows, Severus pushed my slaves aside and stormed into the room—where he came to an abrupt halt.

I felt as if he wavered for a moment, as though he were plagued by the same dizziness that had been tormenting me all night. Or perhaps it was simply due to the horrific sight that he'd lost his balance; either way I couldn't blame him. Even for a long-serving soldier, such a terrible bloodbath among civilians was not an everyday sight.

For a moment Severus seemed perplexed, but then his features darkened. "The gods have taken vengeance!" he announced. His voice suddenly sounded like that of a rioter in the forum. "The immortals will not tolerate sacrilege against them!"

He looked around at his legionaries for approval. The two men hastened to agree with him loudly. Both were still young lads with naked fear written all over their faces.

In the next moment, before I realized what was happening, Flamma had stepped in front of Severus. The former gladiator towered over the centurion in height and breadth like a bull over his calf, and threatened him with a clenched fist. "You blather about the wrath of the gods? Yet it was you who nurtured a deadly hatred for Paulus! And certainly for the druidess, too, did you not?"

Accusingly, Flamma pointed his left hand at the two corpses, while he tensed his right even more and swung his fist dangerously close to Severus' chin.

The centurion did not retreat, but was visibly at a loss for a retort. He may have fought gloriously on the battlefield, but in a duel against Flamma, he would certainly have lost. He knew that as well as any other man in the room.

Flamma now let his anger run wild. "Do you think I didn't notice the way you looked at Paulus?" he hissed at the centurion, threatening him even further with his fist and massive body. "Do you think I couldn't hear what you were saying to your legionaries, behind closed doors and yet loud enough for everyone to hear your invective? How you mocked our god?"

To the legionaries' credit, I must report that they did not abandon their centurion. They rallied closer around him, albeit hesitantly. They stood there on wobbly legs, as if they were braving the rage of the sea god on the deck of a ship.

They glared at Flamma, probably wanting to signal their readiness to fight, but he seemed unimpressed. I had no doubt that he would strike if Severus or one of the soldiers provoked him in the slightest.

XIII

I could not allow any more blood to be spilled!

I took heart and stepped between the disputants—but before I could bring the men to see reason, one of the Celtic warriors intervened. I think it was Cobanix, but one could never be sure, what with the resemblance between the twin brothers.

"The centurion is right." He turned to Flamma with a challenging tone. "It was Paulus who brought disaster upon this house. You know as well as I do that our druids give due respect to all the gods. We are not atheists!"

His brother stepped next to him to give him support. When he spoke, his eyes were on me. "Forgive me for saying this, Thanar, but tonight I thought your cook didn't know his business. Or that something was wrong with the wine. A strange nausea befell my brother and me and confused our senses."

He touched his head as if to give emphasis to his words. "But I was mistaken. The kitchen slaves are not to blame. It was demons that pursued us—dark forces that this apostle brought under your roof, Thanar! They bewitched our senses because they sought Divicia's life!"

"How dare you!" shouted Flamma. "It was you who bewitched our senses! Your sorceress made us dizzy and made us see things that did not exist! But we came together in prayer. None of us had the opportunity to murder your witch!"

Granis and Cobanix rushed toward Flamma as one man. That a fight to the death did not break out between the three of them in the next moment was not my doing. I must confess that to my shame.

I was no longer master of my senses. The evil spell that both the Celts and Flamma spoke of—I too had succumbed to it! Violent dizziness seized me, my stomach rebelled, and my knees felt as soft as those of an old man.

It was Morann who showed incredible courage, and bravely threw herself between the men. She sprang directly in the way of her warriors and held out her open hands to Flamma. They came to rest on his chest—where they looked as tiny as the hands of a child—and yet they seemed to cool the gladiator's anger on the spot.

"Stop, Flamma, I beg you!" Morann spoke softly and without a tremor in her voice, which I could only admire. "There's no point in spilling any more blood!"

Flamma seemed almost gigantic in front of the delicate little woman. Nevertheless, her words touched him. He lowered his fists, snorted something unintelligible, but then let himself be soothed when Morann continued to speak to him.

I could not understand what she was saying to him, as her voice had dropped to a whisper. But I saw that in the gaze with which she looked at Flamma there was more than just the desire to make peace. She felt a tenderness for the former gladiator, I could have sworn.

The two Celts disapproved of Morann's interference; that was written all too clearly on their faces. Nevertheless, they too obeyed the young woman. Close behind her they came to a halt and limited themselves to punishing their opponent with hateful glances.

"She's right," Severus cut in, suddenly quite the voice of reason. Had he remembered that in Marcellus' absence he was the senior Roman officer in the room, and that it therefore fell to him to represent law and order?

But where was Marcellus, I asked myself on this occasion. The slave I had sent out for him had not yet returned.

"It will not bring the dead back to life if you, blinded by revenge, kill each other as well," Severus said. He did not quite manage to mask the thirst for blood that shone in his own eyes. Still, he spoke with some authority. "And both deaths have already been avenged, it seems."

"What do you mean, Roman?" asked Granis and Cobanix, as if from the same mouth.

Severus was clearly enjoying his new role as spokesman for the law. He straightened up to his full height and announced, "Well, isn't it obvious? If it wasn't the gods who struck these two down in holy wrath, they certainly killed each other! They probably got into an argument about ... what do I know, perhaps some detail of your vile cults!"

"Sorry, centurion, but that's impossible." It was Layla who spoke up.

"Impossible, you say?" New anger flared in Severus' eyes. That a woman, of all people, had contradicted him clearly displeased him.

Layla took a step toward forward and gave him a conciliatory smile. "If the two of them went at each other with weapons, and then they both succumbed to their wounds, there should be a sword in this room, shouldn't there? Or at least a dagger. Something with which they inflicted the wounds on the opponent. Can you detect such a weapon, Severus?"

The centurion's gaze darted across the floor, but he could only confirm what I myself had already noticed. Far and wide there was no weapon visible, not even the tiniest knife.

I caught a glance from Granis. The Celt was blatantly eyeing the sword hanging from the centurion's belt. The two legionaries also carried their blades.

This did not escape Severus. On the contrary, he took this demonstrative look as a new insult. He twisted the corners of his mouth. "A soldier of the Empire faces his opponents in fair combat. Man against man. We are not cowardly assassins who kill unarmed civilians."

The way he said it, it was clear that he quite believed the two Celtic warriors could do such a deed.

At the moment Granis and Cobanix were unarmed. Nevertheless, I remembered that they had also come to my house with swords, deadly weapons made of the best Celtic steel.

I myself possessed an extensive arsenal of weapons, which I kept unlocked inside my house. A few particularly beautiful pieces, which had belonged to my ancestors, adorned the walls of the atrium; others I kept in a chamber in the cellar. Anyone could have used them freely if he did not want to resort to his own weapon.

Layla was right; it had to be a third person who had murdered Divicia and Paulus. And this murderer was one of us, because the weather conditions had made it quite impossible for an outsider to have entered my house.

What had driven the killer? It was up to me to find out.

The bloody deed had been committed under my own roof. So I stepped forward and promised the survivors that I would solve this crime. "And Marcellus will then bring this beast to his just punishment!" I added.

The two Celts seemed satisfied with this. Flamma nodded as well. Severus shrugged his shoulders and looked disapproving, but I did not care.

"Tonight, mourn the dead," I continued. "Tomorrow we will set about finding the culprit, or culprits." *When the curse of this night has been taken from us, and hopefully we will all be masters of our senses again,* I added to myself.

I tried hard to sound confident and determined—but at the same time, a part of me refused to acknowledge the bitter truth. A murderer was among the guests of my house yet again.

Only a few months had passed since I had first been confronted with solving a series of murders. Insidious acts of blood, which had found their climax under my own roof.

Was I cursed? Had I myself turned the gods against me in some way? Why else had they once again brought death and destruction upon my house?

XIV

I lacked the strength to think about this question tonight. It would have to wait until tomorrow, just like the investigation I had to conduct. My skull was pounding, and I could have fallen asleep on the spot, standing up.

Caecilia and Philomena, who until now had been kneeling by the Christian's body and shedding endless tears, rose as if at a silent command.

"If you will permit, Thanar," Caecilia turned to me, "we will lay Paulus out in the prayer room. He cannot stay here."

She avoided looking at anyone, but I knew what she was trying to say: *he can't stay here, in the druid's room.*

I nodded, turned and sent a servant to fetch linen cloths to cover the dead.

The way the snowstorm was raging outside, the two dead people would not get the burial they deserved any time soon. *However it might be customary among the Christians,* went through my head. I also did not know the rites of the druids.

The Celts decided to leave Divicia's body in place—on the couch that had served as her bed when she'd been alive.

Flamma took it upon himself, among the Christians, to carefully lift Paulus's body and carry it out of the room in his arms.

My servants were on hand to help where help was wanted. I myself left the room, together with Layla. No one paid any attention to us. Both the Christians and the Celts seemed relieved to finally be rid of each other and to be able to devote themselves to mourning their dead.

Two men had not shown up yet: Thessalos, the doctor—and Marcellus! And that even though I had already sent a slave to fetch him quite a while ago.

"We should go check on him," I said, turning to Layla.

She stood beside me in the hallway, lost in thought, and didn't seem to have heard me.

"What is it?" I asked.

"These murders don't make sense," she said.

A remark that, in its turn, made no sense to me. Did she expect that the lunatic who had committed this bloody deed was a man of reason? Someone who had acted in a logically calculated manner?

"Let's find Marcellus," I repeated. I was starting to get worried about my friend.

"Marcellus," she whispered. It sounded like an echo of my own words.

"Is there something wrong with him?" I asked in alarm.

"Huh? I don't know. When I left him, he was fine."

"But?"

"He—" She hesitated. She seemed to have to search for the right words first, which was entirely out of character for Layla. "He wasn't the man I know, tonight," she whispered. "And something strange happened, earlier, when we were both asleep."

"You mean even stranger than this double murder?" I muttered. I was startled at how bitter my voice sounded in my own ears.

But Layla didn't seem to notice. "There was someone with us," she continued. "A strange phantom. It appeared out of nowhere. And then it spoke to Marcellus."

"Someone invaded your bedchamber?"

"Yes. That is, no. I think he ... how shall I put it, he just appeared, on the spot. You know?"

I did not understand. What did she mean by: *he just appeared*?

"Who was it?" I asked. "Couldn't you recognize him? Was it a man or a woman? Do you think it was the one who killed Divicia and Paulus?"

I couldn't help my voice suddenly being loud and full of worry. An intruder in Layla's room? Was she in danger too, and in my house of all places?

"I don't know. I can't even swear whether I really saw the figure, or whether it wasn't merely a mirage. Oh, Thanar, what on earth has come over us? Did you hear the others? They too complained that something was confusing their senses, didn't they? It certainly wasn't your food, I know that! And Marcellus was equally affected. One moment he felt intense nausea, the next he was suddenly seized by—"

She faltered, averting her eyes. "He was very passionate all at once." She spoke so softly now that the darkness in the hallway seemed to swallow her words.

I laughed—and my laugh sounded hard and bitter, like my words before. "Passionate?" I repeated. "That's not surprising."

She raised her eyes and looked at me questioningly.

I resisted the impulse to brush a strand of dark hair behind her ear that had fallen in her face. "You don't have to go easy on me," I said. "I know how much Marcellus desires you. What man wouldn't?"

She smiled modestly. "Still, tonight was different," she said, "very different than usual. At least, that's how it seemed to me."

Her voice died away. But right after that she added: "I haven't been myself in the last few hours either. My head hurts, along with my eyes. It seems to me that I perceive everything more clearly than usual, as if the colors were more intense, the shadows darker. The voices louder. Even in the evening, when I was reading Caecilia's book, I felt as if the snowstorm were howling in the middle of my head. Do you think the gods have cursed us, Thanar?"

"I've been asking myself the same question," I replied before I could stop myself. I didn't want to worry Layla any further. She wasn't usually jumpy or easily rattled in any way, but now she seemed vulnerable.

Nevertheless, I wanted to get to the bottom of what had happened in Marcellus's bedroom. I had to know who had dared to enter there and what he had been up to.

"I don't think he wanted to kill us," Layla said when I inquired further. "It would have been easy for him, because we were both fast asleep, Marcellus and I. But suddenly—it seemed to me that we startled up almost at the same moment. And then he was standing there. At first I couldn't see him at all. I only heard his voice. Or hers. It didn't sound like it was from this world, you know? And they said they were a messenger from god—the Christian god."

I had to remember that I, too, had had a vision. In my own bedroom, of Iduna, my beloved wife. I had not only recognized her voice without a doubt, but had also seen her clearly in front of me. But I did not reveal that to Layla. Instead, I asked, "And what did that voice want to tell you? Marcellus heard it too, I suppose?"

Layla nodded. "The voice spoke to Marcellus. It said, "The Lord has chosen you, legate."

"The Lord has chosen you? And what else?"

"That was all. I still saw the flutter of a bright robe, then the figure disappeared into the darkness as abruptly as it had appeared."

"And Marcellus? How did he take it?"

"He was spellbound, didn't speak a word. He just grabbed my hand and then ... then I must have fallen asleep again."

For a while, the two of us stood in the hallway in perplexed silence, then I gave myself a jolt. "We should go check on your legate," I said. "I don't understand where he could be."

XV

To my great relief, Marcellus was well. Or rather, he was alive and visibly unharmed; otherwise, he really didn't seem to be himself.

The slave I had sent to wake him a good while ago was just about to help the legate dress. When the young fellow caught sight of me, he huffed an apology for not having returned yet. But one look at Marcellus was enough to know that it was not my slave's fault.

I almost did not recognize my friend. His movements normally showed great strength and body control. Now, however, Marcellus stood before me on wobbly legs and seemed to have the greatest difficulty pulling his tunic over his head. His eyes were shining feverishly and beads of sweat stood out on his forehead.

"Thanar," he growled when he saw me. "Tell me it is not true, what this fellow claims!" He pointed his chin at my slave, who was half contorting himself in order to help Marcellus into his tunic. The lad had to support him with both arms, or the legate would have certainly lost his balance.

"I'm afraid it's true," I said. "Two murders ... a terrible bloodbath. But what happened to you, my friend?"

"I don't know," Marcellus groaned. "My skull feels like it's about to explode at any moment. What a night!" He rubbed his temples and looked at Layla, who eyed him anxiously.

"Divicia is ... dead?" he said after his tunica was finally in place. Paulus's fate seemed to concern him far less.

I nodded. "And her companions hold you responsible for her murder," I added.

My words achieved the desired effect: they shook my friend up. Marcellus blinked, but then seemed to be able to rid himself of his stupor. At least partially.

He looked me in the face and his eyes suddenly seemed a little clearer. Nevertheless, he said nothing, but only mumbled something that sounded like a curse.

"The disgrace affects us all," I said. "You, who thought Divicia and Paulus were safe, but equally Divicia's guards, who themselves failed to protect her and are probably enraged because of that. And of course me, as the master of the house. Two murders under my roof!"

No matter how many times I repeated it, I still couldn't believe it.

Marcellus looked somber. He seemed to be thinking about something, but at the same time great sorrow was visible in his otherwise pleasing features.

I motioned to the slave to leave us alone. Layla stepped close to Marcellus and touched his shoulder.

"Divicia meant a lot to you," she said softly. It was an observation, not a question. And if she felt jealousy regarding this fact, she did not betray it with any expression.

Marcellus did not deny it.

"I noticed the way you looked at her," Layla continued. "And she at you.... It may have been a while since you were close, but she still desired you. And I can understand why you were attracted to her. She was a remarkable woman. How I would have loved to learn from her, her wisdom, her secret arts...."

"Did they kill each other?" Marcellus asked gruffly.

"No," I said. "We didn't find a weapon in the room. That means the killer is still among us."

"We must bring him to justice!" Again, Marcellus rubbed his temples. His skull seemed as sore as mine. "By all the gods, what's the matter with me?" he grumbled.

"It has come upon us all," I said. "An evil spell, a curse of the gods, I don't know. Some it hit harder, others less. Let's hope the haunting is over when dawn comes."

Marcellus headed uncertainly for the door, but I held him back. "Get some rest, friend. There is nothing more we can do tonight. Let our guests perform their rituals, mourn their dead ... and we should try to get some sleep. Tomorrow we'll bring the person responsible to justice. I swear to you!"

Layla put her hand on Marcellus' arm and escorted him back toward his bedside. I took my leave and retired to my own room.

I feared that I would not find any sleep, given the terrible events of the night. But the exact opposite was the case; I lost consciousness as soon as I'd crawled into bed. The remaining hours until dawn I slept so soundly that ten men could not have awoken me.

XVI

The new day had barely dawned when I awoke from sleep, drenched in sweat. I didn't know what had roused me. A noise? A bad dream from which I had been startled awake? I couldn't remember anything. My head ached, and my heart was hammering in my chest.

It felt as if I had not spent the last hours in the realm of Morpheus, the god of sleep, but had descended into the underworld, where usually only the dead found their way.

My throat was parched. I emptied the water carafe, which as usual stood well filled next to my bed, and thirsted for more. My stomach also rebelled, as if I hadn't had anything to eat for days. Which was a good sign, after all. Dead people were not plagued by hunger.

It took me quite a while to get my bearings. The events of the night seemed so unreal to me; misty chimeras in the gray light of the morning. Yet I knew that I had not dreamed them.

Iduna, my deceased wife, who had spoken to me ... followed by the terrible double murder of Paulus and Divicia. Plus the evil spell that had apparently settled over my guests and me: all our senses had gone crazy.

Then there was the messenger of the Christian god who had appeared in Marcellus's room and announced to him that he had been chosen. Was there a connection between these events? Or were the gods merely punishing us as they pleased?

Cautiously I climbed out of bed. I wish I could have said that sanity and clarity had regained the upper hand in my mind with the dawn. But still the ground rolled and swayed under my feet as if I were journeying on the high seas.

I slipped on a robe and stepped out into the hallway. My path first led me to Marcellus's room, although it was not he I longed to see: I needed to speak to Layla. Perhaps she knew more than I did—as was almost always the case. Perhaps she had already been able to solve the first part of the mystery in the early morning.

I knocked on the door of the room, but nothing moved. So I peeked in cautiously.

Marcellus slept like the dead.

There was no trace of Layla.

I woke up the legate. There was no time for sleep now; we had two murders to solve. I touched Marcellus on the shoulder and spoke to him, carefully at first, then louder, and finally I almost had to yell at him to get him awake.

"Where's Layla?" I asked him, after his eyelids had barely opened a crack.

He looked around. "I don't know," he mumbled dazedly. He scrambled up on his elbows, looked around again, and rubbed his temples. "Are they really dead? Divicia and Paulus?" he asked abruptly. "Tell me I just had a terrible nightmare!"

I shook my head. "No nightmare."

Marcellus groaned. His eyelids closed again. I thought he would be overcome by sleep again, but the next moment he said, "The God of these Christians—he spoke to me last night."

"I know. Layla told me."

"I'm supposed to have been chosen...."

The visit of the ghostly messenger, whoever he might have been, seemed to have made a deep impression on Marcellus.

I pondered for a moment, but had to admit to myself that I hardly knew anything about my friend's belief in the gods. Of course, as legate of the legion, Marcellus participated in all public festivities. He sacrificed to the gods as custom demanded, sponsored festivals and games himself, but whether he privately adhered to one of the numerous cults that were widespread in the Empire and beyond—we had never talked about that. And now he was suddenly supposed to be chosen? As a Christian?

It made no sense. But the whims of the gods had always been unfathomable to us humans.

At that moment, one of my slaves appeared in the doorway. "Excuse me, master," he groaned breathlessly, "Layla sent me to look for you."

I jumped off the bed, on the edge of which I had settled. "Where is Layla? Is she all right?"

The slave nodded. "She's over at the—" He faltered, seeming to search for the right words.

"Over at? Over where? Speak up, man!"

"In the chamber you have given to the Christians, master. For their ... rituals." The way the lad looked while uttering these words, he was clearly thinking of all the atrocities that were told about the Christians: incest, cannibalism, dark magic....

"I'll go to her," I said. "You make sure Marcellus comes

around, please."

"I'll be right there," Marcellus moaned. His eyelids were still closed, but he now held his head in his hands as if he were suffering great pain.

I left him to my slave and hurried to the Christians' prayer room. I met Layla in the hallway, just outside the door—and was immediately on the alert.

She had propped herself up against the wall with one hand and stood slightly bent over. Her eyelids were flickering.

The door to the Christians' prayer room was open. One of my slaves was busy mopping the floor. Between the shards of clay of a broken amphora a yellowish liquid had spread, from which a bad smell emanated, as from a latrine.

Layla approached me with an uncertain step and gave me a short, shy smile. She seemed relieved to see me.

"What happened? Are you all right?" I asked her.

"I just feel a little dizzy. When I close my eyes, lights still dance behind my eyelids, like they did last night."

She pressed the heels of her hands against her temples and took a deep breath. "Is there no end to this evil spell, Thanar? And why aren't your servants affected by it?" she added the next moment. At this, she already seemed far less dazed. In general, she possessed a razor-sharp mind and excellent powers of observation—and thus perceived things that others would never have noticed.

She was right; I had not observed in any of my slaves the strange drowsiness, dizziness or nausea that had afflicted me and my guests. Just like that lad who was nimbly and deftly mopping the floor at our feet, all my servants had performed their duties well last evening and during the night.

At least, as far as I could judge. However, I was not yet awake enough to make sense of what this might mean.

"What are you doing here so early in the morning?" I turned back to Layla. "Couldn't you get any more sleep?"

Her smile widened. "I did get some sleep. I remained in the library for some time, dozed for a few hours, but then my curiosity got the better of me, I'm afraid. So I decided—"

"In the library?" I interrupted her before she could continue. "What brought you there in the middle of the night?"

She tilted her head and looked at me sidelong in amazement. "Don't you remember, Thanar?"

XVII

"Remember? Remember what?" I felt a little obtuse. My mental clarity was probably still in a bad way.

Layla looked disappointed. "You can't have forgotten...."

I shivered. Following a spontaneous impulse, I stepped toward Layla and pulled her into my arms. The storm was still howling around the house, but her body was soft and warm.

She lifted her head and looked me in the eye. "So you do remember." A new smile played around her lips.

I didn't have the slightest idea what she was talking about. And I knew Layla well enough that I was certain of one thing: I couldn't fool her. She saw through me without fail. And so it was now. I didn't have to say anything.

Gently she slipped out of my arms and took a step back. At the same time she didn't take her eyes off me. "You couldn't sleep," she said, "after we parted in Marcellus's room. So you went to the library. And it was the same with me. I couldn't get any rest either, my thoughts ran in circles. I got up and wandered through the house, then into the library as well. There I found you. You can't have forgotten that, can you?"

I frowned. My senses had been clouded. They still were. I couldn't have said what they had made me believe last night—and what had been real. Paulus and Divicia were dead, of that I was sure. But that I should have visited the library in the last hours of the night? And had met Layla there? I had no memory of that.

She continued, in a softer voice, visibly unsettled: "We had both come to the library to distract ourselves with some reading, but then ... you must remember that, dearest!" she cried, seized by sudden passion. "I found shelter and security in your arms. I longed for that very much, after all that had happened."

She raised her head and looked me directly in the eyes. Her pupils were large and black as night. "We made love ... like we used to, remember? That's when I first realized I'd missed you. Your closeness, your hugs."

"*We made love*?" I repeated as if in a trance. I felt the urgent need to pinch my arm. Was I still dreaming? Was the divine Morpheus holding my senses captive?

Layla looked at me expectantly, but I couldn't find the words. For a while—it seemed like half an eternity—we just stood there, only half a step apart, looking at each other.

"I don't regret what we did," Layla finally said. "Still, I think it's better if Marcellus doesn't know about it. He wouldn't understand."

I had no idea what to say in response. I had no memory of making love to Layla in my library. And that only a few hours ago?

Obviously, dark forces had taken possession of my house and confused all our senses last night. But I should have remembered a night of love with Layla! Nothing and no one could bewitch me so much to make me forget something like this.

There was a tenderness in Layla's eyes that I had sorely missed. She hadn't looked at me like that for months. Apparently she had enjoyed our lovemaking in the library—

even if it had never taken place. She must have dreamed our encounter. It was a mirage that she thought was real. Had she mistaken me for Marcellus? Or had she just imagined everything from beginning to end?

What could I do? I couldn't let Layla believe that we had made love. Or could I? Was this my chance to win her heart back?

Once again I had to think of my wife, who had stood before me in the flesh that night, a visitor from the realm of the dead. I could have sworn that she was real and very much alive. Had it been my inner longing that had put the strange words in her mouth? That I should reclaim Layla for myself?

Was it all part of the cruel game of the gods? Had the immortals played Layla just as badly as they had played me? But the illusion she was under had to mean that deep inside she longed for me. Or not?

I decided not to fool Layla. If there was a chance that we could get closer again, I didn't want her feelings to be based on an illusion. On a lie, if I kept silent now.

I pulled her back into my arms, stroked her hair ... and told her the truth.

"Just a dream?" she murmured when I had finished. She looked at me strangely, which she often did. Layla was a master of cryptic looks. I didn't call her my black Sphinx for nothing. But that was all she said. She just seemed to be brooding.

"It was a very strange night," I said. "I've never experienced anything like it."

She nodded slowly. "And it gets weirder. Come with me, there's something you need to see. That's why I sent the slave out to look for you earlier. It seems we've all been taken in by another illusion. I can't explain it any other way."

XVIII

Layla's voice had changed; gone was the tender undertone. Now I had Layla the puzzle solver in front of me, who could hardly wait to tell me about a new discovery. She was eager to talk me through a particularly tricky problem.

She led me over the threshold into the room I had put aside for the Christians to pray in. Paulus's body had been laid out not far from the small altar that he himself had arranged. He lay on a low couch, hidden under one of the linen cloths I had provided.

The slave who had cleaned the floor finished his work and disappeared. I had not yet asked Layla what mishap had happened here and what the stinking contents of the broken amphora had been. But neither did I get the chance to enquire about it now.

Layla led me directly in front of Paulus's body. Its outline was visible under the shroud, like the hills of a landscape buried in snow.

"After our, ahem, encounter in the library, which I must have only dreamed, I didn't want to go back to bed," Layla said. "I decided instead to devote myself to the mystery. These murders."

A few months ago, this statement might have surprised me. But by now I knew that Layla had an almost morbid penchant for crime, that she enjoyed nothing so much as solving a murder case.

The thought briefly occurred to me that we possibly owed it to this strange passion that the gods had once again brought violence and death upon my house. But I did not get to contemplate this further, because Layla was already in the middle of a lively description of her morning investigations. She seemed to feel much better now, no longer as weak and dazed as I had found her when I arrived.

"I wanted to take a closer look at the two dead people," she explained to me. "To do that, I first went to Divicia's room. I found Morann, who must have fallen asleep next to her mistress's bed. She was startled when I entered. The room smelled of fine incense, and a myriad of candles surrounded Divicia's corpse. A few of them were still burning. From the looks of it, Morann had performed the last rites for Divicia alone. Maybe only an adept is allowed to do that, and that's why the two men didn't have access?" Layla looked at me questioningly.

I shrugged. I knew the exact customs and rites of the druids as little as Layla did herself.

"It didn't occur to me to ask Morann about it," she said to herself in a reproachful tone. "What's wrong with me?"

I didn't give a reply. There was no answer to this question—which concerned all of us. At least, not yet. I fervently hoped that we would soon find out who or what had bewitched us all. And I prayed to the gods that the mirages and chimeras would not return when night fell again.

"Morann would not allow me to touch Divicia's body," Layla continued. "It was already consecrated to the gods and prepared for its final journey, she said. The touch of a mortal would undo all that. But I could convince her to lift the cloth

Divicia was hidden under a little. That way I could at least get a look at the corpse."

"So, were you able to spot anything unusual?"

"I counted three knife wounds in Divicia's chest."

I nodded. That was nothing I hadn't expected.

"The wounds seemed random to me," Layla added. "They didn't look like the work of a skilled assassin who knows exactly which places to hit in order to kill."

"And what about Paulus?" I asked, pointing to the corpse right next to us. "Was he killed in the same way? It must have been the same attacker, right?"

"You won't believe me," Layla began, but then fell silent and seemed to have to first search for the right words.

I did not press her. Silently, I told myself that after the night that was behind us, I was ready to believe just about anything.

"When I got here from Divicia's room," Layla finally continued her report, "halfway down the hall I heard a loud clang. The kind of sound when earthenware breaks."

"The broken amphora?" I asked.

Layla nodded. "I quickened my steps—and found Caecilia just stumbling out of the room here. Behind her on the floor, I saw the shards and the spilled liquid."

"Caecilia? What's got her in such a tizzy?"

"I didn't get a chance to ask her that, unfortunately. She howled, put her hands in front of her face and didn't seem to notice me at all. She collapsed before my eyes, writhing on the floor—and the next moment she ran away. She left the broken vessel behind. One of your slaves, who came by a little later, volunteered to clean up the shards and mop the floor."

"Very strange. What could have gotten into Caecilia? Was she also tormented by one of those strange visions that haunted so many of us last night?"

Layla tilted her head. "Possibly. But I think it's more likely that she discovered something in this room that scared the hell out of her. Something that's not a mirage."

With these words, she pulled the shroud covering Paulus's body down to his loins, exposing his torso. "Perhaps that was what so disturbed Caecilia."

Layla pointed her index finger at the dead apostle's exposed chest. "After Caecilia fled, I decided to do what I had come to do. I went to look at Paulus's body. And look what I discovered!"

I took a step closer and looked down at the dead man. At first, my aching eyes just casually wandered over the corpse. But in the next moment I realized that something was very wrong.

Paulus lay curled up, half on his back, but with his legs turned to the side. *What a strange way to lay out a dead man*, went through my mind.

His mouth was open a crack. The lips were slightly bluish, and the tongue peeked limply but strongly swollen out of the mouth. The chest of the dead man, however—on which my eyes searched for the stab wounds inflicted by the murder weapon—was completely unharmed!

XIX

That couldn't possibly be! I looked more closely, half expecting that I had been dreaming with my eyes open again. But the sight that presented itself to me did not change.

"No puncture wounds," Layla said, as if repeating my own thoughts.

"But that's not possible!" I cried. "The divine Mercury is playing one of his deceitful games with us!"

Layla's forehead was in deep wrinkles. "He was guiding the hand of a particularly insidious murderer! I think Paulus died in truth by poison, not by a sharp blade," she said. "Look at his tongue, master, how swollen it is. And then the contorted posture."

She now sounded like a medic, expertly making a diagnosis. Only occasionally did she still call me *master*, as she had done back when she had still been my slave. That only happened when she was very excited and not paying attention to her words.

She bent low over the slumped dead man and sniffed his lips. "There's a strange smell he's giving off. Doesn't that also indicate poisoning?"

I was far from ready to follow Layla's new theory. *Poisoned*?

"Maybe Paulus was stabbed from behind and not from the front?" I ventured.

That had to be the solution to the riddle!

"I'm sure we'll find wounds on his back," I cried with confidence. I tried to recall the sight that had presented itself to me during the night.

The room had been half in darkness, and I had not been master of my senses. Moreover, I must confess to my shame that I had avoided looking too closely at the gruesome scene.

Nevertheless, I had a reasonably clear picture of Paulus's body before me. He had been lying on his back, and the chest of his tunica had been bloodied. Just like Divicia's. So I had simply assumed that he had been stabbed from the front.

Now Paulus's body had been washed and rubbed with fragrant oil so that his skin shone and no more blood was visible. The dead apostle was dressed only in a loincloth. Only on his arms could be seen the cuts left by the attacker's blade. Just like on Divicia's limbs. Both victims had fought back against their killer, albeit in vain.

"There are no wounds on his back either," Layla said, "I already had a look."

I didn't miss the chance to check it out for myself. None of us could trust our senses at the moment.

It was not difficult for me to push Paulus up a bit by the shoulder, since his lower body was already lying there twisted to the side.

Of course, Layla was right once again. Not the tiniest scratch marred the dead man's back. But on this occasion I realized something else. "Was it you who twisted his body like that during your examination earlier?" I asked Layla.

She shook her head. "No, I found him in that exact

position."

And already she was voicing the thought that had just occurred to me: "That must mean that he was still moving after he was laid out here, right?" she said. "After he was washed and anointed. His followers certainly didn't put him in such a contorted position, and they certainly wouldn't have left his mouth open like that either. So he couldn't really have been dead at that point. It only looked like it. It wasn't until later that night that he succumbed to the poison—or whatever actually killed him. It was probably only a few hours ago. His body is still warm, feel it."

She gave me a look as if to prompt me.

"It's okay, I believe you," I said quickly.

"He would be cold and clammy if he'd already died last night, wouldn't he? Corpses cool down, become rigid. Not even your exquisite heating here in the house could have prevented that."

Sometimes her cleverness was quite sobering to me. Or maybe that conclusion was obvious, and it was just my mind that still felt like it was packed in a thick fog.

At least, Layla no longer spoke of the wrath of the gods that had befallen my house. She seemed to assume that we were dealing with an earthly perpetrator. With a murder case—which she obviously intended to solve.

"That means Paulus wasn't stabbed at all," I said slowly.

"I don't think so. Someone must have doused him with blood to make it appear that way. Maybe with Divicia's blood? So we found two dead bodies covered in blood, both with cuts on their arms—and jumped to the most obvious conclusion, that both had met their end in the same way."

"But why fake it?" I interjected. "What did the murderer want to achieve thereby?

Layla did not answer me. Her eyes darted around the room, as if to make sure she hadn't missed even the slightest clue.

"Maybe he did it so he could put the druid's body next to Paulus's?" she finally said. "Maybe he *wanted to* make it appear that both had fallen victim to the same murderer. And at the same time! In doing so, he implied a religious motive that may not have been there. Remember the vessel we found in the brazier: Divicia's magic medicine against the plague. Perhaps the murderer was merely interested in destroying that vial?"

"But that has nothing to do with Paulus. Why kill him if the murderer was merely interested in the medicine?"

Layla shook her head in frustration. "You're right, it doesn't fit. But still, why destroy the medicine?"

I shrugged. "If only I knew. Perhaps the assassin had something against Divicia's plan to free druidism from the imperial ban?"

"Hmm." Layla was not convinced.

And essentially, neither was I. My overstimulated brain was just spitting out the first theories it could somehow put together. At least, that's how it felt.

The fact remained, however, that the two religiosi had been killed. Both Divicia and Paulus had been leaders of cults that were met with nothing but hatred from many people. Paulus had almost fallen victim to an angry mob in Vindobona.

Layla tried another theory. "Maybe someone found Paulus

poisoned. He might have been dying, and maybe the person prematurely believed him to be dead. This unknown party might have seen this as an opportunity to kill Divicia as well, and then set up the scene we witnessed. The punishment of the gods that had apparently come upon your house, Thanar."

"There is another possibility," I said after thinking about Layla's words for quite a while.

"Yes, master?"

There it was again, this long since inappropriate form of address. Layla's dark eyes looked at me expectantly. Her expression betrayed extreme tension and concentration.

"Perhaps Divicia poisoned Paulus," I suggested, "in the course of the long conversation the two of them had that evening? Just think back to how they hated each other at first, when Paulus arrived here. And the very next day they were the best of friends? And so animated in conversation that they couldn't stop? What if this sudden sympathy was just fake? If Divicia wanted to kill Paulus, all she had to do was mix some kind of poison into his wine. As a druid, she surely carried a supply of herbs—including some of the dangerous kind."

"And one of Paulus's followers took revenge for this outrage by stabbing the druidess in turn?" asked Layla, "After finding the apostle dying?"

"Exactly. That would at least make sense, don't you think?"

"Well, yes ... but how exactly did it happen?" Layla objected. "Divicia poisoned Paulus—and then stayed in her room with him until he collapsed? Until one of his followers showed up and found him? That would have been very foolish behavior for a murderess, wouldn't it? I, in her place, would have sounded the alarm at that moment when she thought Paulus was dead. To then pretend to be deeply shocked and totally clueless about his death. Something like that, anyway."

"Maybe he wasn't dead just then," I proposed. "Divicia may have measured too small a dose of the deadly poison. After all, Paulus obviously did not die until the early hours of the morning. You yourself noticed that his body was still warm. Divicia, as a herbalist and healer, would surely have been able to recognize that he was still alive last night in her room. Perhaps that was why she wanted to wait before sounding the alarm. She had to fear that he would come to again and then accuse her. She probably didn't expect one of Paulus's followers to show up in her room. But that very thing happened, and this person immediately avenged the apostle's death."

"And which follower would you say it was?" asked Layla. "Someone who went to see Paulus armed with a knife—and immediately turned on Divicia, blinded by a thirst for revenge, when he thought the apostle dead?"

"Hmm. Actually, only Flamma can be considered for such a role," I had to concede. "Caecilia or Philomena definitely not." And even the former gladiator wasn't such a hothead, I had to admit to myself. Not to mention the fact that Flamma no longer carried a weapon, since he had become a Christian.

"I'm afraid we're missing something," I said sullenly to Layla.

She agreed with me—but nevertheless I had the

105

impression that her mind was working incessantly behind her beautiful forehead. Was she developing another idea that she didn't want to share with me yet?

She crossed the room once more, walked to the window and looked out through the pane of glass, behind which only the monotonous white of the winter day could be seen.

She remained there for a moment, deep in thought, it seemed to me.

Then she turned with a jerk and walked back to the place where the slave had earlier cleaned the floor.

"Why did Caecilia come to Paulus this morning with this vessel?" she asked me. "It must have slipped from her hands when she noticed the changed position of the corpse— which must have scared her to death. But what did she want with it? I think that this amphora contained urine. Or something similarly malodorous."

"Maybe it's part of one of those strange rituals that Christians are so notorious for," I suggested. "We'll ask Caecilia about it later, all right? And as for Paulus's cause of death— I think Thessalos should take a closer look at his body. As a medicus, he might be able to tell us what kind of poison the Christian really died of."

"Where is he anyway, our medicus?" Layla replied. "He didn't show up at all last night when we found the dead, did he?"

For a moment she seemed unsettled. She didn't say it, but I knew what she was thinking. Whatever had been seen—or not seen—over the last several hours could have been a mirage. Just like our supposed act of love in the library.

I took Layla by the hand and led her out of the room. I told the first slave we met to go in search of Thessalos and to bring the doctor to me as quickly as possible.

XX

The slave returned much later. I had retired with Layla to my smaller dining room. We were just about to fortify ourselves with bread and cheese when he came stumbling over the threshold.

"Thessalos ... we have found him," he gasped. "Come quickly, master. He's more dead than alive!"

Layla and I jumped up at the same time—although something in my head refused to take note of the slave's words.

Not another death, was all I could think. Was my house really cursed, then?

The next moment I felt ashamed of this self-centeredness. How could I think of myself when Thessalos—whom I considered a friend—was obviously in need?

We followed my slave through the arcades of a peristyle garden. My house had several such leafy, Roman-style courtyards. In the summer, I enjoyed stretching my legs under the shady arcades, engrossed in conversation with Layla about books, philosophers, or distant lands, with the splashing of fountains in the background.

Now, however, we crossed a desert of ice. Plants, fountains, statues—everything lay buried under a thick blanket of snow, and it was only thanks to the industriousness of my slaves that it was still possible to cross the courtyard dry shod, at least under the protection of the arcades. Two of my strongest lads were busy with shovels and brooms to get rid of the snowdrifts that threatened to take possession of the porticos. Meanwhile, new snow was still falling from the sky.

The slave who was leading us stopped abruptly. "We found the medicus over there, master, at the foot of the well."

He pointed with his hand into the middle of the masses of snow, in the center of the garden. "That's where he was lying. Half buried by the snow—so we almost missed him. He must have spent most of the night out here."

In this weather? What had gotten into the young medicus?

"Is he alive?" I asked. "Where have you taken him?"

The slave inclined his head toward the passage we were heading for. "Into the bath house, master. We thought warm water would be the best way to thaw him out."

I nodded and quickened my steps. In my bathhouse there was a plunge pool that could be heated wonderfully—so hot that you could get scalded if you weren't careful.

Among the men of my people, it is considered effeminate to indulge too often in the pleasures of bathing, but I must confess that I was rather fond of this Roman delight.

On the steps of the basin lay Thessalos, surrounded by three slaves who were pouring warm water over him, rubbing his limbs and at the same time infusing him with a steaming drink. Judging by the scent it gave off, it was well-heated honey wine.

Thessalos was conscious, thank the gods! The eyes of the medicus turned to me as I knelt beside him, but he seemed to look straight through me. A beatific smile was playing around his lips. "The griffin! Did you see him, Thanar? A truly regal specimen! Oh, how many years have I dreamed of glimpsing one. Even as a small boy...."

His words were lost in an unintelligible babble, as if he had actually turned into a toddler.

Quite obviously, Thessalos spoke in delirium. Was he close to death and therefore no longer master of his senses? Or had he become another victim of that evil spell full of mirages and chimeras that had afflicted so many of us in the night?

"I think he's had enough of bathing," I said. "Dry him off and wrap him in warm blankets!"

My servants did as they were told. They placed Thessalos on one of the comfortable couches in the neighboring room—the heat chamber, which was called the tepidarium by the Romans—and covered him from his toes to the tip of his nose. Nevertheless, the doctor's lips were still stained bluish, as were his fingertips and feet. But he seemed to have regained some strength.

He was a healthy man in his prime. He had gotten some nasty frostbite, but he wouldn't die on me—at least, that's what I hoped. But what had driven him to leave the house during a snowstorm? What had he been up to in the peristyle garden in the middle of the night?

The next moment he seemed to have fallen asleep. His eyelids flickered, but his breathing was regular. He began to snore softly.

Only a few moments later, however, he jumped up from the couch with a sharp scream. His gaze wandered. When he spotted me, his eyes fixed on mine again. He grabbed my arm.

With amazing strength, his fingers closed around my wrist. "Kykeon!" he cried. "That must be it. Beware the skull, friend, or you're doomed!"

His breathing was heavy. His eyeballs rolled back, then his neck muscles seemed to let him down as well. He sank back onto the couch like a lifeless doll. The next moment he was already asleep again.

I looked at Layla. "By all the gods ... do you have any idea what he was trying to tell me?"

Layla did not seem to have heard me. Her gaze was fixed on the once again peacefully slumbering figure of the doctor. She looked as if she had sunk into deep thought again. Only slowly did she raise her head—and then shook it. "Not the slightest idea, master."

XXI

Layla and I kept vigil at the doctor's bedside for a good hour, and he seemed to have fallen into a deep sleep.

He was breathing regularly, and even his feet and hands were slowly regaining a healthy rosy color. In a few hours, I hoped, he would be responsive and would be able to conduct an examination of Paulus's body. Perhaps his expertise in poisons would help us to track down the murderer.

In the meantime, I decided to start questioning the residents of the house. If we could determine who had been where and in whose company at the time of the murders, we could certainly narrow down the number of suspects a bit.

As a first step, I gathered my house slaves and also my trade assistants and guards who were not traveling at the moment and questioned them, together with Layla.

Some of them had been up until the early hours of the morning to serve my guests. And slaves are quite perceptive fellows; they hardly ever miss anything. Some of them are not afraid to eavesdrop on a conversation or secretly observe a scene that is certainly not intended for their eyes. So I hoped to get valuable information from this source concerning the nocturnal activities of my guests.

I learned the following: Granis and Cobanix, the two Celtic warriors, had indulged in a game of dice late into the night, just the two of them in their room. They'd emptied a good number of amphorae of wine that my servants had served them. "We would certainly have noticed if one of them had left the room for a longer period of time," the slaves in charge assured me.

Three of the Christians had sat together in their prayer room, another lad asserted. Flamma, Caecilia, and Philomena, however, had not indulged in the pleasures of Bacchus, but had devoted themselves to pious chants, invocations to their god, and the study of some scrolls and codices. None of the three had left the room for more than a walk to the latrine, the slave claimed.

Severus the centurion had been seen in various parts of the house, but at no time near Divicia's room. He had checked on his legionaries, who were staying in the servants' quarters, and all three had apparently made rounds in and around the house. Thus they had probably fulfilled those guard duties that Marcellus had imposed on them.

To no avail, I thought bitterly. In any case, they had not been able to stop the murderer.

Another slave tried to make me believe that he had been watching the corridor in front of Divicia's room for several hours, right up to the time when the two murder victims were found. He claimed to have devoted himself to cleaning work in that part of the house, a duty that had actually been due during the daytime. He swore to me by all the gods that no human had approached Divicia's room, apart from the house staff, who had supplied the two cultists with drinks.

The way he looked, it was clear to me what he was getting at. *No human.* He seemed convinced that Divicia and Paulus had died at the hands of the gods. Or by some evil spell. His fear-filled protestations remained rather vague in this regard.

He had probably taken a nap in a quiet corner while performing his duties, I thought to myself. However, I refrained from telling him that to his face.

Layla, on the other hand, seemed to take him quite seriously. She interjected several questions while he spoke. When he had finished, she sat there lost in thought and once again looked mysterious, as only she could.

"Let's find Marcellus," I said to Layla after we'd finished the slave interrogations. Surely the legate would want to actively participate in the investigation. He must have fallen asleep again early this morning, instead of joining us as promised. Hopefully, he was by now completely in control of his senses again.

While we walked along the corridors to his room, however, I had to admit to myself that my own senses were far from being their best. My head ached, and if I moved too quickly, that awful rocking and swaying of the floor, with which I had already had to struggle last night, set in again. But at least in the bright light of day my deceased wife did not appear before my eyes once more.

We found Marcellus engrossed in conversation with Morann. At the side of the young druidess sat the two Celtic warriors, arms folded and stone-faced. They looked like two guardians from the ancient epics I loved to read: sinister, hostile, and now fiercely determined to protect Morann at all costs, which they had failed to do for Divicia.

"How do we proceed now?" Marcellus said just as we

entered the room. "Will you make the journey with me and prove to us the effects of your plague remedy?"

Morann was about to answer, but stopped when she caught sight of Layla and me.

"You can speak freely before them," Marcellus said. "Both enjoy my full confidence." He gave me a curt nod, and I breathed a sigh of relief to see him back in full possession of his powers.

One of the two Celtic warriors puckered his face. A silent, but nevertheless clear message that he would certainly not trust anyone anymore, not even the master of the house.

Morann, however, gave me a timid smile. Then she said, "Divicia entrusted me with the secret of the plague remedy. I can make new powder, but not here. Only in our sanctuary can I find the necessary ingredients and equipment. Besides, the council must first be consulted as to whether, after Divicia's death—" She hesitated.

"Speak frankly, I pray you," said Marcellus.

"Whether the council thinks it wise to make the offer to the Emperor once again, as Divicia had decided to do, after her mission came to such a terrible end."

"Are you going to be Divicia's successor?" Marcellus asked her straightforwardly.

"I am in no way worthy," Morann said. Her answer came quickly, too quickly. Apparently, it was important for her to demonstrate humility and modesty.

After a moment of silence, however, she added, "That, too, will be a decision of the council. I am sorry to say that there is no one in our sanctuary who is anywhere near as advanced as Divicia in the sacred arts."

"You were her most important student ... and right-hand woman, weren't you?" I said. "So it's quite likely that the council's choice will fall on you."

Morann humbly bowed her head, but said no more.

"We will solve Divicia's murder. And execute the guilty one, I give you my word," Marcellus said—as if this were nothing more than a routine official act for him. I can't say that I could relate to or even share this confidence.

"I thank you," Morann replied with another nod of her head. Her tone was polite and did not betray the slightest emotion.

She turned and addressed me, "May we stay under your roof, Thanar, until the guilty party is found?" she asked. "When we return to our people, we would at least like to be able to bring with us, besides Divicia's body, the consolation that the outrage has been avenged."

"Of course," I said quickly. "And I, too, give you my word that we will bring the murderer to justice. Divicia died as a guest of my house. It is my sacred duty to avenge her death."

XXII

When Morann and her two protectors had left us, I informed Marcellus of the morning's events.

With as much detail and structure as I could, I described to him the observations we had made on Paulus's body. I then went into what had happened to Thessalos during the night. "If we had found him just a little later, you would now have to look for a new camp doctor," I concluded my report.

"Do you think he, too, was the victim of an attack?" asked Marcellus.

"I think he was a victim of that dark spell that took possession of all of us last night. His senses were confused, he spoke something about a griffin, which he had apparently seen. Perhaps he followed this mirage into the garden—and lost his senses there? In any case, he is outwardly unharmed, and we could not discover any traces of a struggle. Neither in the peristyle nor on his body."

"I don't understand what came over us," Marcellus said somberly. "Something so strange has never happened to me before. How is a man to fight against an enemy who has such magic at his disposal?"

Layla, who had been pacing up and down the room, merely listening to what I had to say, settled down on the sofa next to Marcellus and took the floor. "Thessalos spoke of a skull—of which he warned us strongly—and he used a strange word: Kykeon. Can you make anything of it?"

"*Kykeon*?" Marcellus asked incredulously.

Hope seized me. "Yes. Don't tell me you've heard it before?"

"Indeed I have," my friend replied. "Though in a very different context. It is truly not something I would associate with Christians or druids."

"Don't keep us in suspense," I cried.

Marcellus furrowed his brow. "Kykeon is a sacred brew, used in the mystery cult of Eleusis," he said. "I'm not an initiate. A friend from my youth told me about it, only very vaguely. Initiates are forbidden to talk about the rites on pain of death."

"Eleusis?" I repeated. By name, probably everyone knew this cult. It had originated in Greece—Eleusis was not far from Athens—but had spread throughout the empire. Even if predominantly in the east.

The mysteries revolved around the goddess Demeter, as well as Persephone, her daughter, who had been abducted by Hades into the underworld and had to spend half of each year there. However, I did not know more about the cult—just like Marcellus, if one could believe his words.

"Are you sure?" I asked him. "About this kykeon?"

He nodded. "It's a potion with a top-secret recipe, that much I know," he said. "Thessalos is Greek. Perhaps he is an initiate of the Mysteries and that is why he hallucinated about this brew?"

"And the skull? Is it also part of the rituals of Eleusis?" I asked.

Marcellus shrugged. "Not that I know of. But as I said, I'm not familiar with the details of the cult."

"Perhaps the mirages the medicus saw were related to these mysteries?" suggested Layla. "The griffin he was chasing?"

We looked at each other helplessly, then I said—trying not to let us all sink into gloomy brooding—"Well, we'll find out. As soon as Thessalos regains consciousness, he can explain to us what the skull and this kykeon are all about."

"Right," affirmed the legate. "In the meantime, let's take a look at the suspects, my friend. Have you already been able to find out who has an alibi and who doesn't?"

I gave him the statements of my slaves, but added that I had not yet spoken myself to the guests of my house—our murder suspects.

"Good," said Marcellus, to whom it must have seemed quite natural that I had waited for him with regard to the interrogations. Full of energy, he jumped up and wanted to hurry out of the room.

Layla, however, held him back by placing a hand on his arm. "Can I be there," she asked, "for the interviews? I want to help solve these murders."

Marcellus and I exchanged a silent glance. Of course, this was an incomprehensible request for a woman. But we both knew that Layla was no regular woman; whether we wanted to admit it to ourselves or not, her needle-sharp mind would be of great help to us. Because the murderer we had to hunt down was also damn smart—and moreover probably in league with dark forces!

So, as if from the same mouth, we agreed, and Layla smiled as contentedly as a cat to whom we had slipped a bowl of milk.

"There is something that worries me," she resumed our conversation. "If Morann knows the secret of the plague remedy, don't you think she might be in danger now, too? After all, maybe the murder wasn't about Divicia or Paulus. What if the killer just had something against Divicia's mission? What if he wanted to prevent her from using her medicine in the service of the Empire?"

"Can we be sure that this magic remedy has really been destroyed?" Marcellus objected. "You have found a broken vessel. And some scattered powder. But who will tell us what it really was? What if someone stole the medicine and destroyed another jar with a powder in it to mislead us? Maybe theft was the motive for the murder of the druidess?"

"How useful would it be to steal the magic remedy if you don't know the secret of its recipe?" I retorted. "Divicia would not tell us a word about how to prepare this powder. And neither do we know how exactly to use it on plague sufferers. I don't think she would have revealed that knowledge to any outsider."

"Hmm," Marcellus grumbled. "Not even if he threatened her life?"

"I rather think the Christian was the actual murder victim," I said. "Someone poisoned him. I think we can say that much for sure, although Thessalos has yet to confirm it. Maybe Paulus's killer was merely surprised by Divicia. Perhaps she became an unwilling witness to the crime?"

"But since they both died in the end," Layla said, "I guess neither a Christian nor a Celt is our killer. Right?"

Which left only one of the Romans: the centurion Severus or one of his men. Perhaps all three together. Maybe they had acted and killed the sacrilegious before the wrath of the gods fell upon Vindobona.

I shied away from expressing this thought openly in front of Marcellus. However, the way his facial features darkened, he seemed to have come to this conclusion without my help.

He didn't like the idea, that was clear. "Someone could have killed Divicia out of revenge," he said, promptly coming up with a new theory. I had long since lost track of how many we had by now, each sounding as unsatisfactory as the next.

"To atone for Paulus's death," Marcellus added. "Someone from the Christian camp. Most likely the gladiator."

"Just because he's a battle-hardened man?" I objected. We all knew that women could be equally treacherous killers. Although they were more likely to use a poisonous potion than a sharp blade, normally. But what was normal about such a heinous double murder?

"But if Divicia was killed in revenge, that would mean, by implication, that one of the Celts must have murdered Paulus," Layla said. Sometimes she already sounded like an advocate or a judge.

I contradicted her, "Maybe the Christians merely assumed that one of the Celts was the culprit."

Which brought us back to the Romans, to Severus and his legionaries as the most likely culprits. The circle had closed. And we hadn't made any progress, it seemed to me.

"Let's start the interviews," Marcellus said. "The Christians first."

XXIII

We chose a smaller dining room as the place for our tribunal. I had some appetizers prepared, along with warm wine.

The afternoon was already well advanced, although the time of day could hardly now be determined. The snowstorm had subsided in the meantime, but my house was literally buried under the mass of white, and now we were also enveloped in thick fog. Like a shroud that the gods had spread over my property—a sign that we were all doomed.

With a few hearty sips of wine, I tried to dispel these morbid thoughts. I turned my attention to Caecilia, Paulus's freedwoman, who had taken a seat opposite me.

Marcellus, with Layla at his side, had made himself comfortable on my right. Caecilia was the first one we were interrogating. Like a slumped heap of misery, she sat before us with her eyes lowered.

Layla took the floor, while Marcellus was visibly still pondering how he should begin the interrogation. "You seemed distraught, Caecilia," she said straightforwardly, "this morning, when I met you in the prayer room with your dead apostle."

When she wanted to be, Layla could be the most sensitive woman in the world. But she also knew how to get to the point briefly and without beating around the bush. Apparently she had seen an advantage in that for this conversation, or rather, for the interrogation. Nothing seemed more important to her than finding out the truth.

Caecilia abruptly raised her head and glared angrily at Layla. The impression of a hopeless heap of misery was suddenly gone. How did they do it, these women folk? Was each of them blessed with the qualities of a chameleon that could undergo a complete transformation from one moment to the next?

"I seemed distraught?" hissed Caecilia. "Was I supposed to laugh and dance, perhaps? Paulus is dead! He was a prophet, a holy man, an apostle of the Lord. And I was privileged to serve him. How will I ever get over this loss?"

Layla switched to her gentler mode. "I'm sorry for your pain, Caecilia. And your loss."

Marcellus and I had not yet spoken a word in this interrogation that *we* had wanted to conduct. And it did not look as if we would get the opportunity to do so any time soon.

Layla was already continuing: "May I ask you something, Caecilia? That amphora you took to Paulus this morning—what did it contain? It gave off a, um, somewhat strange odor, if I may say so. Did it serve any of your Christian rituals?"

A somewhat strange odor was a very euphemistic way of putting it. Whatever might have been in the amphora—from the remains that had spilled over the floor, the acrid smell of a poorly cleaned latrine had risen to my nose.

Caecilia didn't seem to understand what Layla was talking about at first. But then she nodded. "It's a tincture that keeps away the evil spirits that might otherwise take possession of the dead person's soul. I admit it's not a Christian custom, but something I picked up from my own family."

She didn't seem willing to tell us anything more about it. She remained silent and looked at Marcellus.

The latter would certainly have had some questions for the Christian, but Layla did not give him the opportunity to ask them. Her eager sleuthing had probably made her forget all the rules of politeness. Marcellus, on the other hand, who would have had no problem asserting himself against any man—whether verbally or in a physical duel—let her have her way.

Layla continued, "Tell me, Caecilia, did you notice that there were no puncture wounds on your prophet's body? That he had certainly not been stabbed? Was it this discovery that gave you such a shock this morning? That made you flee the room as if out of your mind?"

"It was an evil spell of this demon worshipper that took Paulus's life!" Caecilia replied heatedly. "You're just wasting your time here, pestering me with questions."

She clicked her tongue disapprovingly. I felt as if I were watching a wrestling match between her and Layla, these two former slaves who otherwise had nothing in common.

"None of us has wielded a dagger against this witch," Caecilia said in a sharp voice. "We spent the whole evening together in pious devotion, Philomena, Flamma, and I. In the prayer room where Paulus's cold corpse now rests," she added with bitterness. "We studied the Sacred Texts—an essential part of our faith. And we pleaded with our God to protect us from the evil that has befallen us at Vindobona."

"Your god must have let you down," I interjected. I couldn't resist the biting remark.

"No one is able to fathom the ways of the Lord. He

sacrificed his own son for the sins of the people," Caecilia returned. Her tone sounded so unctuous that I felt provoked.

Layla, meanwhile, was not deterred, and continued her questioning. "Flamma, Philomena and you—so you were together all evening? All those hours between dinner and that time Philomena found the dead?"

"I already told you that." Caecilia fixed her gloomy gaze on me. "Why don't you ask your slaves, Thanar, if my word means nothing? They served us all evening. They brought us wine and bread, and oil for the lamps.... There was always at least one of them on hand when we needed something."

Her forehead smoothed out. The aggressiveness with which she had met Layla seemed to have departed from her for the moment. "Your servants' zeal for work is quite excellent, Thanar," she added after a brief pause.

Layla, however, didn't let up. "Surely one or the other of you visited the latrine at least once, didn't you, Caecilia? And left the room briefly to do so."

"Yes, of course. Each of us went at least once to the latrine that night. But just as quickly, we all returned."

Caecilia fell silent. Her eyes wandered around the room, as if she had to think about something she couldn't comprehend.

"Philomena was on her way to the latrine when she found the dead," she finally continued. "Anyway, she said she was going to relieve herself when she left Flamma and me. She stayed away quite a long time, but of course we didn't worry about it. We couldn't have guessed...."

"That she would find two dead people?" I said.

Caecilia nodded wordlessly. Her eyelids twitched as if she were about to burst into tears. She looked tired, hopelessly defeated. As if she had long since cried her eyes dry.

Layla exchanged a look with Marcellus that I didn't know how to interpret.

XXIV

I jumped at the opportunity to finally take the conversation with Caecilia into my own hands.

"Philomena could have stabbed Divicia—before she supposedly found the dead and raised the alarm," I said. "Instead of seeking out the latrine, as she claimed to you, she may in fact have attacked the druidess. She would have had plenty of time for that murder. And Paulus was poisoned—at least that's what we assume. Perhaps quite some time before Divicia died. Thessalos will help us in this matter as soon as he regains his strength. He can probably—"

"Has something happened to the medicus?" Caecilia interrupted me. Her lips quivered. Did she know more than she was admitting?

"Thessalos merely suffered a mishap," I said quickly. "He got lost in the snow, almost froze to death ... but he is already on the road to recovery. Soon he will be responsive, of that I am sure."

"And you say that Paulus was poisoned?" Caecilia continued.

"Probably. Do you know something about it? Were you able to observe anything suspicious? Who might have given him a poisonous potion or some deadly food?"

When she did not answer me, I urged her, "You must not be silent, Caecilia! You want Paulus's death to be avenged, don't you?"

She remained silent, but seemed to be deep in thought. I could have sworn that she knew something.

Layla had suddenly become equally silent. I understood it even less, since she had thrown herself so courageously into this interrogation at the beginning. She looked as if she were thinking secret thoughts that she didn't want to share with us. Her forehead was deeply wrinkled, but a soft smile played around her lips.

Did she enjoy interrogating murder suspects? I wouldn't have put it past her. I already knew that she loved solving crimes and mysteries.

Marcellus, meanwhile, seemed to have gained the same impression as I had regarding Caecilia: namely, that she knew more than she was letting on. He rushed to my aid. "I can tell something is on your mind, Caecilia," he said in the commanding tone of a general. "What is it?"

The Christian woman gave him an awed look. Then she shook her head—only to contradict herself immediately with an affirmative nod. Still her lips quivered. "It's just," she began hesitantly, but then spoke no further.

Marcellus leaned forward a little, and I did the same.

Caecilia spoke so softly that I could barely understand her. "Philomena," she said, only to fall silent again. She lowered her eyes, clasped her hands in her lap, and began to knead her fingers like bread dough.

"Keep talking," Marcellus demanded. "What about Philomena?"

Caecilia swallowed. "She ... she used to fill her husband's cup. And she always prepared his meals. Here in the house, too, she took over. He was not to be served by slaves, but exclusively by her. A service of love—that's what she called it. If he was really poisoned by food or drink, she would have had to...."

Caecilia fell silent again—and now shook her head violently. "But no!" she exclaimed, her voice suddenly far stronger. "That is unthinkable. Surely Philomena would never harm her husband!"

"How did things go in their marriage?" I interjected. "Were they happy together?"

I didn't know Paulus very well, but in the years I had done business with him, his wife had hardly ever made an appearance. And he had never spoken of her either. I had gained the impression that, although the two of them kept up a friendly relationship, they each led a life of their own. As is usual in many—if not most—marriages.

Caecilia did not give an answer at first. The thought that Philomena might have had something to do with Paulus's death seemed to frighten, no, to shock her.

Finally she spoke: "I think Philomena liked to be the wife of the argentarius. But not so much that of the Christian apostle. The abuse that Paulus—and therefore also she—had to endure in Vindobona put a lot of strain on her. Philomena is a respectable woman from a good family. Her reputation is very important to her. And I also believe that she did not like the meager life that Paulus led since his conversion."

"Did his business suffer so much from his conversion to Christianity that he had to cut back?" Marcellus asked, astonished.

"No," Caecilia replied, "but our God praises poverty."

Marcellus looked at her in silence for a moment, then shook his head uncomprehendingly. I could only agree with him. What was good about suffering lack?

"One more question," Layla spoke up. "Yesterday afternoon I witnessed—quite by chance—an argument. Between you, Paulus and Philomena. I was a little taken aback by that, given that you stand for brotherhood and charity in your faith."

Caecilia didn't seem to grasp—or want to grasp—what Layla was talking about.

But my black Sphinx probed relentlessly. "You were in the courtyard, just behind your rooms. An undisturbed place for a conversation, I imagine, albeit very uncomfortable at this time of year. You were standing together under the arcades, and you were getting quite angry with each other, it seemed to me. Surely you haven't forgotten that? So what was this argument about?"

"Oh, that," Caecilia said snidely, pretending to have remembered that insignificant conversation at that very moment. "It was about the upcoming trip, with the witch, where she was going to demonstrate her dark magic. After all, Paulus had decided that we should go with you to demonstrate the power of *our* God. The only God who commands life and death, and—"

"What was there to argue about regarding this trip?" I interrupted her. I was in no mood to endure another religious lecture.

"Philomena and I—we were scared," Caecilia said straightforwardly. "We wanted to talk Paulus out of it. I mean, traveling toward the plague, that's a terrible idea. But Paulus reminded us that we mustn't doubt, that God is watching over us and will protect us from all evil. Which is true, of course. It was no argument, then, just a ... rebuke that Philomena and I deserved." She narrowed her eyes, seemingly ashamed.

I wasn't sure I bought her story. Marcellus, however, seemed satisfied with the explanation. He dismissed the Christian woman and decided to continue with the questioning after dinner. It was getting late; the darkness of night had long since descended upon my house.

XXV

"Do you think Philomena poisoned her husband?" Marcellus asked, taking the floor as we gathered around the richly set table in the dining room.

None of the other guests had shown up yet, so we could talk freely amongst ourselves. However, we did not wait too long to eat; I was quite hungry, and my friends seemed to feel the same way. We had our cups filled and feasted on the delicacies that were ready for us.

"I could picture Paulus's wife as a murderess," I said to Marcellus, "from what Caecilia has told us. Philomena—as one of only a few people, from what I have judged so far—had the opportunity to commit both murders. And I see a motive, too. I can well imagine that she did not want to be married to the Christian preacher and ascetic that Paulus had turned into. The opportunity was ripe to kill him here under my roof. She could blame it on the Celts, or your men, Marcellus. Plenty of choices."

"That's true," my friend agreed. There was a hard, grim expression in his gaze.

"Here's how it might have happened," I continued. "Philomena poisoned her husband's food or drink. She had ample opportunity to do so, as she always used to prepare his food. And Divicia saw her do it, quite unintentionally, I suspect. I don't think she was spying on Philomena. Why should she? But Philomena, for her part, might have noticed that there was a witness to her murderous deed. Then she had no choice but to kill the druidess as well. She may have stabbed her at the time she supposedly found the bodies. Perhaps Paulus was dying by then, and Divicia accused Philomena of the murder."

"Whereupon the latter silenced her," added Marcellus. "But where did Philomena get the dagger?"

"Maybe she suspected that Divicia might have seen something and was simply well prepared? It's not hard to get a blade in my house. "

Marcellus nodded slowly. "Possibly. That's how it might have happened."

"But the time frame was very short," Layla said. "According to what Caecilia told us, Philomena left the prayer room only for a brief time. Then she was heard shouting because she had supposedly found the dead. If it were she herself who had stabbed Divicia, she should have gotten blood splatter on her robes, shouldn't she? But she would not have had time to run to her room to change. Or am I seeing this wrong?"

"We don't know exactly how long she really was alone," I said. "Caecilia may have misjudged the amount of time."

Marcellus contorted his face in disgust. "What a deed. Poisoned by your own wife! A traitor in the heart of the familia!"

At these words he gazed tenderly at Layla. Surely he thought that she would never do something like that to him. It was true, of course. Still, I felt jealousy at the way he looked at her.

"We should interview Philomena next," I said quickly, trying to mask my discomfort. "Right after dinner."

"Absolutely," Marcellus agreed.

Layla said, "There was also a traitor in the camp of this Jesus. This is what it says in the book of the Christians that Caecilia lent me. One of his disciples betrayed the prophet to the Roman soldiers with a kiss."

"How despicable," Marcellus grumbled.

"What a god," I cried, "who does not even recognize the traitors in his own ranks!"

I expected Marcellus to agree, but he remained silent. He seemed to be lost in thought. Was he thinking about the vision that had haunted him last night? Of the supposed messenger of the Christian god who'd announced to him that he had been chosen?

What had really happened in Marcellus's bedchamber? Had he and Layla been deceived, just as I had been on that cursed night?

Chosen. Could it be at all possible? Marcellus, a Roman legate—a chosen one of the Christian god? And if so, what exactly had this strange immortal chosen him for? Was Marcellus to succeed Paulus? Had this god already foreseen the bloody deed and designated my friend his new apostle?

Or was Marcellus destined for even greater things? Just as Divicia had harbored the highest ambitions for druidism.... Was the legate supposed to obtain something similar for the Christians? A recognition of this cult in the Roman Empire?

My head was spinning. The inconceivable events of the previous night were joined once again by the strange dizziness and nausea that simply would not leave me. I must confess to my shame that at that moment everything seemed completely hopeless to me, until Layla tugged at my sleeve and gave me an encouraging smile. Had she once again read my mind, as she so often did?

"I think some of your guests may prefer to dine in their rooms today," she said as she gestured with her head toward the empty dining sofas in the room. "Would you like me to see to it that something is served to them?"

"I'll handle it, dea—"

Dearest, I had wanted to say. But that was highly inappropriate in the presence of Marcellus. Layla was now *his* sweetheart, no longer mine.

"Layla," I quickly corrected myself—which did not escape her. I earned a Sphinx-like smile, while Marcellus seemed preoccupied with his own thoughts and obviously hadn't noticed my slip of the tongue.

I breathed a sigh of relief. "Thessalos will hopefully feel a return of his healthy appetite," I said. It was the first thing that came to my mind.

I had become so caught up in the desperate attempt to make sense of the events of the previous night that I had not thought about the medicus at all. I had actually intended to check on him before the evening meal.

Well, I would just send some food to his room and then pay him a visit later. He had probably slept through the afternoon anyway, and hopefully found strength in the arms of the god Morpheus.

No one from the Christian camp showed up at the table, and the Celts stayed away, too. So I sent a total of three slaves to provide my guests with food and drink. No one should have to complain about a lack of hospitality on my part—even if my house was already considered cursed.

None of my servants returned. Instead, only a short time later, shouting and clamoring reached my ears through the open door of the dining room.

XXVI

Layla, Marcellus and I were on our feet at the same moment. What was the meaning of this commotion?

Together we hastened out of the dining room. Or rather, we staggered. I suffered a new dizzy spell, so that I had to brace myself against the walls in order not to lose my balance. Layla ran as clumsily as a young dog beside me, and Marcellus squinted his eyes in utmost concentration, probably also in an attempt to keep himself halfway safely on his feet.

My chest tightened fearfully. Had the curse of last night come upon us again? Were the gods playing a cruel game with us?

We followed the shouting, and only a few steps later we had located the cause of the commotion. Some slaves were crowding in front of the Christians' prayer room.

One of my kitchen maids stood crying next to the remains of a roast she must have dropped along with her tray and plate. A mush of broken dishes, meat and vegetables had spread at her feet.

Next to her, a young slave clung to the door frame. His body was stiff with shock, and his hands trembled like those of a very old man. I recognized him as one of the three lads I had sent to take care of the meals for my guests.

Marcellus impatiently shoved the slaves aside and pushed his way into the room. There, however, he also came to an abrupt halt. A sound of horror escaped him.

I followed him—and in the next moment it was clear to me what had caused the renewed commotion in my house: on the floor, between the small altar of the Christians and the couch where the murdered apostle rested under his shroud, I caught sight of Thessalos, the medicus. He was lying on his back, his arms stretched out from his body. The hilt of a dagger protruded from his chest. He was dead.

One of my slaves, probably the most fearless of those present, pushed his way through to me and whispered: "Paulus's wife, master—she was also murdered. We found her next door, in her bedchamber."

"Philomena?" I cried. The ground seemed to break away from under my feet. I just managed to grab my slave's arm, otherwise I would probably have fallen. I felt as if I could hear my own blood rushing in my ears.

Thessalos and Philomena—dead? Two more murders?

I struggled to shake off the dizziness and get a grip on myself again. Just a short while previously, Paulus's wife had been our best suspect for the first two murders. And now, suddenly, we had two more bodies, including hers?

I silently prayed to the gods, imploring them to let me escape from this unspeakable nightmare. *Please, let me open my eyes, safe and secure in my bed, on a sunny spring day.* Or in the depths of winter for all I care. Just without all the corpses!

But nothing happened.

At my feet lay Thessalos, whom I had called a friend. To whom I owed my life. The kind doctor, who had been so highly skilled—murdered by this atrocious beast, whose highest ambition it seemed was to kill my entire group of guests.

We hurried over to the room that directly adjoined the Christians' prayer room, the spacious chamber where I had put Paulus and his wife.

Part of me still hoped that it was all just a bad dream, another delusion that this time my slaves had also fallen for. But I had hardly crossed the threshold of the room when I had to bury this hope for good.

There Philomena lay, half on her back, half turned to the side, on the floor in front of her bed. A fatal wound gaped in her neck.

I looked around, but could not see any weapon. So she had not judged herself after she had murdered Thessalos. She was not our killer—just another victim, like the lamented medicus.

Right next to me, Layla suddenly cried out.

The next moment she was in my arms, her head pressed against my chest, her eyes averted from Philomena's dead body.

A strange surge of emotion took possession of me. I felt concern for my beloved Nubian, but at the same time joy that she had taken refuge in my arms—not in those of the legate, who stood only a few steps away.

"What's wrong with you?" I whispered in her ear.

Tentatively, she lifted her head from my chest and squinted over at Philomena's corpse. In the next moment, she detached herself from me and scurried unsteadily toward the dead woman. She stared at the corpse, blinked, rubbed her eyes.

"It's nothing," she said faintly. "I thought I saw something ... but I guess it was just another mirage."

"What is it?" asked Marcellus. He moved next to Layla and put his arm around her.

She looked first at him, then at me, her eyes dark and large and with a nameless fear in them—which truly did not happen often.

"I thought I saw a demon," she whispered, "a dark beast crouching on Philomena's shoulder, slurping her blood. But now it has disappeared. What is going on with us, Thanar?"

She looked at me pleadingly, then squinted her eyes and shook her head, as if it could help her shake off the terrible curse that held our senses captive.

An icy shiver ran down my spine. I searched for comforting words with which I could restore Layla's cheer, but not a syllable would pass my lips. My throat was as raw as that of a man dying of thirst wandering through a desert.

One after the other, the guests of my house now pushed into the room—those who were still alive. The shouting of my slaves had probably alerted them all. Flamma and Morann came running together, followed by Caecilia, Severus with his legionaries, and finally the Celtic twins. They rushed into the room, but it was far too small to accommodate them all.

Flamma roared when he realized who the dead woman was. His eyes blazed with anger—and if Marcellus had not courageously intervened, it would have come to a brawl. I could not make out, though, who Flamma actually wanted to attack. Was his anger directed at Severus or the Celtic warriors?

Marcellus, in any case, fearlessly jumped in front of the giant—with all the authority due to a legate of the Empire.

"Don't you dare, Flamma!" he shouted. "The law is in my hands. Mine alone! The beast that has raged here will not escape its just punishment. But that right and duty falls to me, no one else. Are we clear?"

I admired Marcellus for this heroism, how he fearlessly stood up to the former gladiator. But it did not escape me that he'd had to summon all his strength for this. He seemed tired, dazed, only a shadow of the imposing commander I usually knew.

Flamma's fists were still clenched. For an endless moment, he stared down at Marcellus, as if he were imagining the most painful way to kill him. But finally he lowered his hands, took a deep breath—and respectfully took a step back.

Severus and the Celts relaxed as well. The centurion's hand had already moved to the sword at his belt, and the Celts, too, would undoubtedly have been ready to engage Flamma in a fight to the death.

Marcellus sent them all back to their rooms, like a pater familias reprimanding his stubborn offspring. Grumbling and swearing softly, but otherwise unresisting, the men obeyed, departing together with Caecilia and Morann.

I returned to the prayer room, to the medicus' body, and carefully removed the blade from his chest. I looked at it more closely.

As I had feared from the first sight of this weapon, it was one of my own daggers, which I kept in my armory, unlocked and accessible to everyone. After all, I had not been prepared for a murderer in the four walls of my own house.

The blade would not tell me who had wielded it, whether Celt, Christian or Roman. Anyone could have used it. We had two more dead to mourn, and yet we were no closer to finding the murderer.

XXVII

Perplexed by recent events, we decided to continue our interrogations. After all, a smaller circle of suspects now remained, as Marcellus grimly noted.

First, however, I asked my slaves and servants when Thessalos and Philomena had last been seen alive.

A lad had found the medicus asleep—but alive—when he had gone to fetch him for dinner. He'd decided not to wake the doctor, but to check on him again later.

So Thessalos must have been killed within the last hour, while my friends and I were having dinner and speculating about the murders. It was the same with Philomena. She, too, had been seen alive shortly before.

We returned to the dining room that we had used earlier in the afternoon for our conversation with Caecilia. Marcellus sent out a slave with the order to bring Severus, the centurion, to us. He was the one we were going to interrogate next.

While waiting for him, we used the time to discuss the two most recent murders.

How sober that sounds. And yet I remember that I could hardly grasp a thought clearly because of all the nausea and anxiety. And as for Layla and Marcellus, they seemed in no better shape than I was. Still, we all did our best to concentrate. We *had to* find a solution.

Our thoughts circled around two possible theories: first,

Thessalos or Philomena—possibly both together, although we could see no connection between the doctor and Paulus's widow—had committed the first two murders. The fact that they now had to give up their lives was in this case possibly an act of revenge, carried out by one of the Christians or Celts.

Or second, the two were innocent of the first two murders, but for some reason had gotten in the way of the killer.

"Here's what I think happened," I said. "Thessalos came to in the early evening. He remembered that we had told him of two deaths during the night. He left his sleeping quarters and went directly to the Christians' prayer room to take a closer look at Paulus's body. And that was exactly what the murderer wanted to prevent. Thessalos would certainly have been able to find out what Paulus had really died of. The murderer lay in wait for the medicus and stabbed him. Surely Thessalos was still very weak and thus practically defenseless."

"And Philomena?" objected Marcellus. "Surely she must have died before the medicus—if we assume that the murderer killed them both with the same dagger. After all, he then left the weapon in the doctor's chest."

"In what order they were murdered, we have no way of knowing," Layla objected. "Perhaps the murderer possesses more than one weapon? But I don't think either Thessalos or Philomena were transported. They were assaulted where we found their bodies. Both were lying in a pool of their own blood, and there were no other blood traces. Neither in the rooms, nor in the corridor in front of them."

"Right," I said. I had also made this observation—and

drawn the same conclusions.

Marcellus took the floor again: "What difference should it make what Paulus actually died of? We already know that he was not stabbed. We are as good as certain that he must have perished by poison. How else, if he had no visible injuries? And the word must have spread all over the house. After all, we made no secret of it. So was it really worth killing Thessalos over it, to risk another murder just to keep the medicus from examining the corpse more closely? That seems nonsensical to me."

"Possibly it is important by *which* poison Paulus died," I objected. "Perhaps it points to the murderer or could at least give us a decisive clue."

"So it must be," Marcellus said. "Or this beast simply enjoys killing. How vile!"

At that moment, Severus entered the room. His cheeks were sunken, his eyes surrounded by dark circles. Like all of us, he seemed to suffer from the curse of the gods that had come over us. And he had probably not slept for some time.

We began by questioning him about the ways and deeds of Thessalos last night. After all, he had shared the sleeping quarters with the medicus. Would he be able to tell us how the physician had gotten lost in the peristyle garden, where he had almost frozen to death?

"Thessalos roused me from my sleep," Severus said. "It must have been perhaps half an hour before the commotion, when the murders were discovered. He was babbling confusedly about some creature that mustn't be allowed to get away from him. What was it? A manticore? No, wait, a griffin—yes, exactly. With those words, he stormed out of the room. I went right back to sleep after he left."

"So he left the room in the middle of the night? After he had already been asleep?"

"Yes, he went to bed early, suffering from nausea. He didn't like his stay here," Severus said, with a sideways glance that was clearly directed at me. "None of us does. When will we return to Vindobona, legate? Do you not see it for yourself? This house is cursed, full of demons and evil spirits that gather around these godless ones. They beguile our senses, want to seize our souls. With their dark spells they incapacitate us."

"Let it go, Severus," the legate said flatly. "Enough of this whining!"

But the centurion was not deterred. The fear that tormented him seemed to have made him forget due respect for his commander.

"They will slaughter us one after the other," he cried fervently, "if we do not get out of here! Thessalos was merely the first among our ranks they've taken, the weakest link, without combat experience. Even if he was a brave lad," he added quickly. It seemed he did not want to offend any of his comrades in the legion, if at all possible.

He spoke quickly, talking himself into a rage. Finally, he stared at Marcellus with a challenging expression: "Look at yourself, legate! You are also only a shadow of your former self! My men and I cannot protect you—not here in this cursed place. You know that we would die for you, fighting man against man! But against these forces we are—"

Marcellus raised his hand and put a stop to his centurion's torrent of words. "You forget yourself, Severus!"

Under normal circumstances, the legate would never have let his subordinate get away with such disrespect. But now he merely said—and in a feeble voice: "Let's get back to Thessalos. Go on with your report, Severus."

As far as my friend's condition was concerned, I unfortunately had to agree with the rebellious centurion. Marcellus' strength was not at its best. And the rest of us were hardly better off, there was no denying that. But nothing and no one would make me flee my own house!

We will hunt down this murderer, if it be our last act, I said to myself with grim determination.

The centurion glowered angrily at Marcellus, but finally complied. "As you command, legate." He clicked his tongue disparagingly. "Well, as I was saying, something roused the medicus from his sleep, he muttered confusedly about a griffin, then he dressed hastily and stormed out of the room. That was the last I saw of him that night. In this life," he corrected himself.

Thessalos had still been fantasizing about the griffin when we had found him half frozen this morning. Had this legendary bird appeared to him as my deceased wife had appeared to me? As Layla had imagined the act of love with me, and she together with Marcellus had believed to have seen the messenger of the Christian god in their bedroom?

Thessalos might have fled from the griffin, or chased after it. He had probably run into the garden, right into the middle of the snowstorm.

I was pretty sure that it had happened that way. But why had the murderer sought Thessalos's life? There was still no answer to that question.

I tried to focus again on the interrogation of the centurion. "So you were alone in the room after Thessalos disappeared, is that correct?" I asked him. "Let's say for half an hour until the murders were discovered?"

He didn't seem to understand why I wanted to know that. But when I continued to talk and asked him where and how he had spent today, up to the time when we had found Thessalos' and Philomena's corpses, I think it finally dawned on him.

Instead of answering me, he turned again to Marcellus. "Am I on trial here, legate? Am I accused of a crime by your ... *Germanic* friend?" He gave me a disparaging look.

"Just answer the question," Marcellus ordered him. "No one is accusing you."

Not yet, I added in my mind. The self-righteous behavior of the centurion was starting to make me angry.

"I spent most of my time with my men today," he finally said—turning to Marcellus. I might as well have been invisible. "We went out to see if we could make our way through the snow. All you have to do is give the order to leave, legate. It's not snowing anymore, and if we all work together, with the slaves of this house, we should be able to make it back to camp."

XXVIII

"What do you actually know of Severus?" I asked, turning to the legate after the centurion had left the room. I didn't like the fellow, and not just because of his boorish manners and the disrespect he showed.

Marcellus pondered for a moment, then shrugged and said, "Actually, he is a capable man. He's been serving in Vindobona for a number of years. Worked his way up to the rank of optio quite quickly, and was recently promoted again to centurion. His family is from eastern Pannonia. Respectable people, as far as I know. He's a superstitious fellow, but then that's true of half the legion."

"And he's never been guilty of anything?" I asked.

Marcellus shook his head.

We continued our interrogations. Next we sent for Granis and Cobanix, but we could get as little useful information from the two Celts as from Severus.

They had seen nothing, heard nothing, and had each spent the times in question, when the murders had occurred, together. Which didn't make for a very good alibi, but that didn't seem to matter to them. They visibly took it as an insult that they were being treated as suspects.

We summarily dismissed them and told them to send Morann to us—expecting that they would return together with the druidess. But when Morann finally entered the room, another man was at her side: Flamma.

The terrible events of the last hours seemed to have forged an even stronger bond between the two. The druidess and the Christian—there didn't seem to be any problem between them because of their very different cults, which was at least gratifying, if rather surprising.

Flamma seemed to be rather strong at present. Whatever was going on in my house—or should I say haunting my house?—it hardly seemed to have affected the former gladiator. He looked a little tired, but otherwise he seemed quite unperturbed.

Morann, on the other hand, leaned against her companion's shoulder as soon as the two of them had taken their seats, and seemed to have great difficulty following our questions, as if she were not really in her right mind, but half asleep.

The interrogation—in which we included Flamma, since he was already here—turned out to be just as unsatisfactory as the other conversations before.

Morann pretended to be as blind and deaf as the two Celtic warriors. Nothing heard, nothing seen ... and also in the run-up to the murders nothing suspicious had struck her.

Flamma was no better. He first repeated what we already knew. He had spent the hours before the first murders together with Caecilia and Philomena in the prayer room.

Today in the afternoon and early evening—the time when Thessalos and Philomena had been stabbed—he had kept Morann company. And neither of them had noticed anything conspicuous during this time.

Because they only had eyes and ears for each other, went through my head.

"I didn't hear any screams—or anything else that indicated a struggle," Flamma said.

Which was probably because no fight had taken place. Philomena must have been overpowered in a flash. We had not found any injuries on her arms that would have indicated an attempt to defend herself, and the medicus must have been equally unprepared for the attack.

Marcellus and I looked at each other. Of course, we didn't say this openly in front of the suspects, but I thought I knew exactly what was going on in his head, that he was thinking the same thing as I: *What now?*

Although we had both dealt with a series of murders before, neither of us was in our element here. Marcellus might be a gifted commander; he was good at leading an army of several thousand men. And he also knew how to manage a legionary camp like Vindobona.

For my part, I was an experienced and successful trader—at least that's what I thought. But when it came to convicting a treacherous murderer, we were both truly fish out of water.

Could we even hope to solve these terrible acts of blood—now four in number? Did we stand the slightest chance against the forces at work here?

I must admit that at this point I was overcome by a deep hopelessness—coupled with a bitter melancholy that choked my throat.

Layla was as inexperienced as Marcellus and I when it came to solving crimes. For her, too, the series of murders that had plagued Vindobona in the summer had been the first and only bloody mystery she'd had to deal with. But she seemed to be born for such challenges, or at any rate, had a special talent for them. Need I mention that it was she who finally asked Morann the right question, the all-important question?

"As a druid, you are also a healer, aren't you, Morann?" she began. "That means you are very familiar with the effects of various herbs, potions, ointments, and powders, right?"

The Celt nodded wanly, but didn't seem to understand what Layla was getting at with this question.

"In the last conversation we were able to have with the medicus before he was murdered, he warned us about a skull," Layla said. "And he spoke of kykeon. According to Marcellus, the latter is a sacred potion used in the Mysteries of Eleusis. Can you perhaps tell us more about it? Could this potion have something to do with the murders? Is this kykeon poisonous if you drink too high a dose of it? We wanted to ask Thessalos about it as soon as he had regained his strength ... but that is no longer possible." The words burst out of Layla, as if she had been eagerly waiting to ask these questions. Now she looked like a bloodhound following a promising trail, one that would eventually lead him to the game he was mercilessly hunting.

A change took place in Morann. She suddenly sat bolt upright. All languor seemed to have fallen from her as if by magic. "Kykeon?" she repeated slowly—as if the word were a powerful incantation that could only be uttered with the utmost reverence. "And Thessalos spoke of a skull?"

Layla nodded. "Can you do anything with that?"

Morann looked at Flamma. In her eyes was an expression of supreme anguish. "Oh, how blind I have been!" she exclaimed abruptly. "How foolish! The curse, the derangement of our senses, which has tormented us for days ... I truly thought that we had turned this god of Paulus against us. Definitely not a good god, but in truth an evil demon. You must believe that, Flamma!"

The gladiator turned away, but did not object.

Morann continued as if in a trance: "Kykeon. This could be it! It *has to be*! This potion could have caused the curse, the visions, the nausea, everything! Such a brew is able to dazzle and beguile, to confuse the senses ... until one can no longer distinguish between what is real and what is an illusion. Surely that was what your medicus wanted to tell you. I, on the other hand—"

She bit her lower lip and clenched her hands into fists. "I have been so clueless! Why didn't *I* come to this conclusion? Divicia would never have missed it! If only she hadn't been snatched from us in such a vicious manner!"

XXIX

"Go on, I beg of you," Marcellus exclaimed. "What do you know about this kykeon?"

Morann pressed her lips together, probably still hard in judgment over herself. She did not seem to hear Marcellus at all. "Divicia, my beloved mistress," she whispered in a brittle voice.

She blinked away a tear shining between her eyelashes. But finally she composed herself; she swallowed hard once more, then began to explain: "Divicia studied the medicinal plants, the brews, potions and spells of many different peoples. And once she spoke to me about this kykeon of the Greeks, in the course of the teachings she gave me. It is a sacred potion that has great power. It is able to open the eyes of us mortals to the world of the gods. In the hands of the uninitiated, it can also be a deadly weapon. And it is only a thin line that separates divine visions from eternal damnation, as is so often the case when one strives for the highest."

She looked into Flamma's dark eyes—he seemed to have long since forgiven her for the abuse of his god and was watching her with undisguised admiration.

The hint of a tender smile flitted across Morann's youthful features. But it failed to alleviate the deep melancholy that resonated in her voice. She continued, "It all depends, with such magic remedies, on following the recipe without the smallest error and ingesting the right amount. And even then, kykeon can cause dark visions, physical nausea—much like our own sacred potion of the sages that we brew from the mistletoe plant, according to ancient recipes as secret as the Greeks'. In the end, when you consecrate yourself to the sacred rites, you can never be sure whether you will find yourself at the feet of the immortals for a few hours, or setting out on a journey of no return, to the world beyond our own. The world of the dead."

She squeezed Flamma's hand, which she had taken in hers during her excited monologue. Then she turned her head and looked at Layla, Marcellus and me. "I'm sure of it," she said emphatically. "Someone has desecrated the sacred kykeon and used it as a weapon against us."

"Not *someone*," Layla replied. "The murderer! So that's how he managed to confuse all our senses, even terrify us, so that he could pursue his bloody goal undisturbed."

"Then he probably killed our medicus for that reason?" Marcellus said. "Because Thessalos recognized the way in which the murderer had put us under a spell, that he'd bewitched us all with that magic potion!"

"And Paulus? He died from a lethal dose of that kykeon, didn't he?" I interjected. "It would not have escaped the notice of the medicus if he had examined the corpse in detail."

"Certainly not," Marcellus grumbled.

Layla made a skeptical face, but said nothing. I couldn't guess what was going on in her head.

"The recipe of kykeon is unknown to me," Morann took the floor again. "The adepts of Eleusis keep it strictly secret. If an initiate reveals anything, he could be punished by death, or that's what Divicia told me. But she believed that through her studies and experiments, and her great experience with the remedies and magic of all peoples, she had discovered the two main ingredients. "

"Seriously?" Marcellus exclaimed.

Morann nodded. "The words of your medicus confirm it—at least in part. Hear me out. I'll get to that in a moment."

"Yes, yes. Go ahead," Marcellus said quickly.

It was good to finally see a spark of hope in my friend's gaze. I shared his feelings; we were on the right track, I was sure of it. Thanks to Morann's explanations, we had come a little closer to the murderer, to this bloodthirsty beast.

The druidess wasted no time: "Divicia was quite sure that the kykeon potion is brewed with the help of opium," she announced, "that intoxicant which can be obtained from the sap of the poppy plant. But the most important ingredient is the *skull*. That's what Thessalos was talking about, wasn't it? My people call it ergot, and it has many other names. It is a demonic black fungus that attacks grain. It has a much greater power than opium. Deadly power, if you don't know how to use it."

Nameless horror seized me at the words of the druidess. With the sleeve of my tunic I wiped the cold sweat from my neck.

But then an idea came to me. "What if Paulus took too much of this kykeon just by some misfortune?" I asked my friends. "Whoever bewitched us with this demonic brew must have mixed it into our food or drink. There's no way he could have foreseen which of us would ingest more of it! So maybe he didn't want to kill Paulus at all?"

"Paulus hardly ate anything, did he?" said Marcellus. "At

least, as far as I could tell. He did, after all, practice moderation in all the pleasures of life since he'd become a Christian apostle."

"That's true," I said.

"But I can't get my head around what this poisoner's intentions were," Marcellus added. "What drove him to risk all of our lives with this skull-poison? This is madness!"

"Also, Divicia was stabbed, not poisoned," Layla added, "just like Philomena and the medicus were. Whatever the original intention of the criminal may have been—he became a murderer, and very quickly. If the curse that stunned and confused us was due to this kykeon, we were first administered it yesterday evening, weren't we? At that time the confusion, the nausea, the visions started ... all that we thought was a punishment from the gods."

The murderer had also fooled us in a devious way, I reminded myself, concerning the death of the apostle. He had made us believe that Paulus had also been stabbed. Like Divicia, whose body had been found next to his.

Even with our new knowledge about the deadly potion, I didn't even begin to understand what had driven the killer. Had Morann's findings not brought us the breakthrough I had hoped for, after all?

"Since last night, we must have eaten or drunk this poison several times," I said to Layla, "because today the curse continued. Even now, I do not feel strong and in good health." *Or in my right mind,* I added in my thoughts.

"You can say that again," growled Marcellus.

The next moment, a new realization hit me. Reflexively, I slapped my forehead. "That's it!" I exclaimed. "Now I understand why my slaves seemed so wholly unaffected by the curse! They do not eat and drink with us, and therefore got none of the murderer's poison."

"Indeed," Marcellus said, and Morann nodded in agreement.

"But now at least we know what we're up against," she said. "And we can take action."

"You can count on it," I replied. No, I solemnly swore it to her; I put all my anger into my words, all my hatred for this murderer who was still hiding from us, this beast who had fooled us so badly. "I will immediately see to it that from now on everything we are served is strictly supervised. Every cup, every plate! No more of these unspeakable poisons that rob us of our senses!"

Marcellus stared into the wine cup, which he had already all but emptied. Disgusted, he pushed it away from him. "I think I will limit myself to water from now on," he said, "drawn straight from the well. Until we've hunted down this assassin!"

In my house, we used to follow the Roman custom of quenching our thirst with wine—heavily diluted with water. There were always well-filled amphorae in the guest rooms, too. It would be all too easy to tamper with them in an unobserved moment.

"One thing, however, I do not understand," Layla took the floor. "The messenger of god who spoke to you, Marcellus ... last night in your chamber. He can't have been a delusion, because we both saw him, didn't we? And I heard the same words you did. How is that possible?"

She did not repeat the divine message in the presence of

Morann and Flamma, but I still remembered it well. Marcellus was supposed to be a chosen one of the Christian god.

"It was not a delusion!" exclaimed Marcellus, before I could say anything. "That messenger stood before me as bodily as ... as all of you do now!" He made a sweeping hand gesture that included each of us. "I swear to you, on my life!"

"You had better not swear on your life, Marcellus," I objected, full of bitterness, "for in my house a life does not seem to be worth much anymore."

He dismissed my words with a gruff gesture.

"Consider what I told you about the kykeon potion—under whose influence you were, legate. No, still are," Morann said. "It is a sacred potion that normally serves this very purpose: to open our mortal senses to the world of the gods. So it should come as no surprise if a messenger of the gods met you and spoke to you."

She fell silent for a moment, but seemed to have something else on her mind. Obviously, she was thinking about how best to phrase it.

Finally she said, "I would be careful if I were you, legate. It may seem an honor to you to receive divine messages. And, of course, no one will be surprised that a god would choose a man like you."

She lowered her head reverently. "Nevertheless, I want to warn you. This god of the Christians is not who he claims to be. He is definitely not well-disposed towards us humans; I hold fast to that conviction. Perhaps it was he who gave one of his adepts the secret recipe of the kykeon—and the vile idea of poisoning us all with it."

XXX

Kykeon. So this deadly intoxicant was the key to the ghastly curse that lay upon my house. It had made us see things that did not exist. Our most secret dreams, but also our greatest fears, had become reality before our eyes. And perhaps an overdose of this poison had cost Paulus his life.

Of course, it was better to take on an assassin who knew the secret of such a potion than to have to defend ourselves against a curse of the eternal gods. Nevertheless, after the conversation with Morann, I felt as if Wodan himself, god of war and death, had turned out to be our enemy. I sat there paralyzed after the druidess—and Flamma—had left the room.

Layla's eyes widened, but whether out of fear or hopeful excitement because we had finally taken a step forward, I couldn't tell. "What do you think, Thanar? Who among your guests might have knowledge of this kykeon potion?" she asked.

"Divicia, of course," I replied, "but she died shortly after we first fell into the intoxication. She could have poisoned us at first, but then the effect wouldn't still have lasted, would it?"

"Morann seems to know quite a lot, too," Marcellus said, "though she may swear she doesn't know the recipe. She was Divicia's favorite student, after all."

"But she wouldn't have told us about this potion if she herself had used it against us, would she?" I objected.

"This could be a ruse," Marcellus said. "These sorcerers, herbalists, poisoners ... they're clever. And devious."

"The druids use their powers for the good of the people," Layla protested. "Divicia spoke of this to me several times when she was still among us. They heal instead of harm."

"I thought so, too," Marcellus grumbled. "At least when it came to Divicia. But her student ... do we really know this woman? Perhaps Morann's fondest wish is to rise herself to the position of her people's high priestess. Maybe that's why Divicia had to die? And the Christian was just an accidental victim of her demonic potion?"

Layla did not answer. She suddenly seemed lost in a dark musing.

"What is it?" asked Marcellus, irritated.

She raised her head. Her eyes had narrowed to dark slits that shone like two pieces of coal. "I just remembered some-thing," she said in a strangely altered voice. "But surely it doesn't mean anything."

"Tell us," said Marcellus.

"The wife of Severus, your centurion ... I just remembered that I know her. Not particularly well, I've met her two or three times at most. Once in the amphitheater, a second time in the thermae of the civilian town...."

"So what?" asked Marcellus.

"She is a midwife, my legate. A healer who knows herbs and potions, spells that relieve pain and cramps, but also the kind of poisons that allow a woman to deliver an unwanted fetus into the realm of the dead!"

"What are you trying to say?" Marcellus seemed incensed. "That Severus could have used her knowledge to brew this death potion? And that he has used it indiscriminately against us all? Including me, his legate?"

He faltered. In his sudden anger, he couldn't seem to find the right words to defend his centurion against the accusations. Or was he not quite so convinced of the man's innocence after all?

"I told you I'm sure it doesn't mean anything," Layla tried to placate him. "I just remembered about his wife."

Marcellus wanted to say something back, but I raised my hand. "Wait," I said, then fell silent and listened. I had heard a noise, outside in the hallway. Footsteps that were quickly moving away.

I rushed to the door, yanked it open. At the end of the corridor one of my slaves appeared. He was not about to leave, but rather coming towards me. Moreover, he was walking barefoot. It could not have been his footsteps that I had heard.

The fellow was loaded with several amphorae. Apparently, he was about to supply me and my guests with new wine, thereby intoxicating us once again—unknowingly, but therefore not less effectively—and put all our lives in danger. Each of these amphorae could contain a new dose of kykeon.

"Have you seen anyone? Here in front of the door?" I snapped at him.

He flinched in fright, almost dropping one of the amphorae.

I paused and moderated my tone. The poor fellow was not to blame for the fact that I had a poisoner under my roof, nor for my suspicion that someone might have been listening at the door.

I explained to the man that I had heard footsteps and that it was probably only thanks to his arrival that the eavesdropper had made off.

"I'm sorry, master. I didn't see anyone," he assured me, bowing his head as if he had been guilty of grave misconduct. "Shall a guard be posted, master?"

"No. It's all right. Maybe it was just some curious soul." Even under normal circumstances, I would catch one of my servants or farmhands with his ear to a door every now and then. I took it rather lightly and never punished such behavior. Household servants were curious, loved to spy. That had always been so.

So I dismissed the fellow, but not before I had given him new instructions concerning the food and drink for my guests. "From now on, only water, freshly drawn from the well," I instructed him. "And tell the others as well. In addition, guards are to be posted at the well, by the pantries and in front of the kitchen!"

The fellow looked alarmed, but swore to me that he would take care of everything right away. With that, he scurried away.

"Were we overheard?" Marcellus asked when I returned to the room.

"I'm afraid so, though I'm not able to say for how long."

"Well, if it was that assassin, we've let him know that he won't have such an easy time with us from now on," he said grimly.

I nodded wordlessly. I can't say I shared Marcellus's optimism. "It's getting late," I said wanly.

"You are right, friend. Let's continue tomorrow," Marcellus suggested. "When the effects of this depraved potion have worn off, which rob a man of his will and senses. How despicable; only a coward would fight in such a manner!"

He slapped the table with the flat of his hand. "When I get my hands on this murderer, he will wish to be torn apart by the beasts in the arena. But he will not have that mercy!"

He jumped up, grabbed Layla's hand and pulled her with him. "Let's go to sleep, Thanar. With nothing but well water to drink tonight, we should be ourselves again in the morning. And then...." He left unfinished the threat against the unknown killer who had played so dirty with us.

He put his arm around Layla, but at the same time leaned heavily on her delicate shoulders. Two nights under the influence of the vile intoxicant with which we had all been poisoned were taking their toll. Marcellus's fighting spirit might be unbroken, but he left the room with the steps of a tired old man.

Layla turned to me once again at the threshold. Our eyes met, but it was impossible to interpret what was going on in her head. Was she longing to spend the night in *my* arms—as the killer's intoxicating potion had led her to believe last night? Was she already regretting that she had made Marcellus her lover? My black Sphinx, she was so mysterious, so unfathomable. She beguiled me like a sorceress, confused my senses no less than that treacherous potion of the murderer did.

I accompanied them to the room that I had given to Marcellus as his bedchamber. He wished me good night with brief words, then disappeared together with Layla. The door closed noisily behind them, and I was left alone in the hall-way. Alone and suddenly very lonely.

Marcellus had omitted to call his men to him and assign them to the night watch. Was he counting on Severus to take care of it? Or was the opposite true? Did he not even trust his own soldiers anymore, and therefore did not give a damn about their nightly guard duty?

I did not try to ask him about it. I returned to my own room and threw myself exhausted on my couch.

XXXI

I rolled sleeplessly—but still haunted by nightmares—on my night bed. The horror images of the last days passed behind my closed eyelids, one corpse after another. I saw so much blood that I thought I would drown in it. I even felt as if I could taste it on my own lips.

I don't know how many hours I had lain there like that, when suddenly a new storm seemed to howl around the house, louder and more frightening than all the weather of the last days.

Drenched in sweat, I rose from my bed. The howling pierced my bones, and it was still swelling. It was no storm, no; it was the terrible call of the wolves!

Was I dreaming again? My wildly beating heart murmured to me that now the end had come. The apocalypse, the final downfall.

Was this another one of those visions, a product of the demonic potion with which the killer had poisoned us?

I had quenched my thirst before falling asleep with nothing but well water, which my good servants had brought as ordered. The howling, however, would not cease, and now it even sounded as if it were coming from inside my house, as if the hungry beasts had gathered in my atrium to feast on the warm flesh of our bodies.

A sharp scream followed, the scream of a woman. I thought I recognized the voice—no, I knew it was her. Layla!

All at once I was fully awake.

I threw on a robe, struggled with it for a moment until I found the arm holes, then rushed out into the hallway. I ran into Layla's old room, located right next to mine. It was only when I found her bed empty that I remembered Marcellus had taken her to his chamber.

I hurried through the dark corridors of my house. Nowhere did I meet a slave who could have quickly brought me a lamp or torch. Had they all gone into hiding, these fearful, superstitious fellows? And this in spite of the fact that only that afternoon I had impressed upon them to assign more guards at night! No wonder the murderer could do whatever he wanted in my house.

The howling of the wolves died away, only to be replaced immediately by a terrible yowl. In addition, I suddenly felt as if I could hear the sounds of a lyre. A delicate, barely audible music.

Damn it, I was still not master of my senses! I hurried on, reaching the door of the room where Marcellus and Layla should have been sleeping. It stood open; I stumbled in, called for the two of them ... and came to an abrupt halt when I almost collided with a wolf. A pathetically whimpering wolf, fleeing in wild panic from something.

But he didn't get far, collapsing as soon as he rushed past me. A last yelp, then the dark bundle of fur lay dead on the floor.

I could not see anything clearly, as no light was burning in the room. Only through the window came the diffuse light of the moon and the stars, reflected by the endless white of the masses of snow that had enclosed my house.

I recognized Marcellus on one of the couches. He had thrown himself protectively in front of Layla, unarmed, but seemingly determined to defend her with his naked fists.

But there was someone else in the room. I thought I saw the outline of a figure in front of me, barely taller than the average human. He seemed to be wrapped in a white robe and was holding a sword in his hands. With it he was lashing at the remaining wolves.

I could still make out three of them, and they retreated with a howl. The third or fourth blow of the figure knocked down another of the animals. And immediately another furry body hit my feet. The animal gasped in agony, then lay still.

I could still hear the music. It seemed to be coming through the walls. A beautiful melody, like the music of the gods. Was it really the sound of a lyre? Or just another deceptive spell that fooled my senses?

The figure struck down another wolf. The last one, if I had counted correctly. In any case, the howling stopped, but the music continued.

Suddenly, a voice spoke to us, echoing like a silver trumpet. "Listen, Marcellus! You are chosen among men. My angels are watching over you. Renounce your false idols and follow me in the true faith! Then neither blade nor claw can harm you. Not even the dark wings of death. I am the highest, the only God."

XXXII

Immediate silence fell over the room. The floor was littered with furry bodies—the corpses of the slaughtered wolves. There was no trace of the figure that had fought off the beasts with his sword. The divine music and the voice that had spoken to Marcellus were equally silent.

I expected to see slaves and guests crowding in the doorway. Surely they must have heard the commotion? But not a soul was to be seen. Apparently, no one had the courage any more to check on my so obviously-cursed house.

I ran out of the room, down the hall, until I reached the kitchen, where a fire was kept burning at all hours of the day and night. The slave who had to guard it was cowering under a wooden stool like a frightened child and crawled out only after I had assured him three times that I was not a demon. I refrained from scolding or rebuking him and quickly lit several lamps myself. Equipped with them, I returned to my friends.

Marcellus sat upright and stiff on the bed. His gaze clung raptly to the ceiling, as if expecting a divine apparition to descend upon him at any moment.

Layla was crouching next to him. She had pulled her legs to her chest and wrapped her arms tightly around her knees. The bloodthirsty wolves, this evil nightmare that had not been one at all—that had probably broken even her courage.

I could not blame her. I myself felt as if a giant worm was eating its way through my guts. I expected at any moment to see the walls of my house collapse, and the hosts of the Christian god storming down from heaven in fiery chariots.

In the light of the lamps I saw what only confirmed what I already knew; I had not imagined the attack of the wolf pack. This time my senses had not deceived me. Four lifeless carcasses lay within rapidly spreading pools of blood on the floor. The stench of their wet pelts and blood rose to my nostrils and choked me.

Finally, life came into my house. Flamma was the first to find his way to us. He appeared in the doorway—with Morann at his side.

A horrified groan escaped the druidess at the sight of the beasts. She whirled around and buried her face against Flamma's chest.

The next moment I caught sight of the tall Celtic warriors, and behind them Caecilia, closely followed by Severus and his men. They were all crowding into the doorway of the chamber now.

The two legionaries looked as if Severus had only been able to drive them from their quarters under threat of death. The centurion himself stood unsteadily on his feet and looked around in confusion. He was holding his head with one hand, and I noticed that he was injured. His arms were littered with ugly cuts. After all the blood, however, that had flooded my house in recent days, these wounds left me strangely cold. At first I did not understand what they might mean.

The legionaries stared at the dead wolves, then over at

Marcellus, awaiting orders, or an explanation for the inexplicable.

But the legate was still spellbound by the sight of the badly-slashed beasts. Slowly he rose from his bed and knelt down next to the largest of the wolves. He looked at the animal's broken eyes and palpated the slack jaws, which were armed with razor-sharp teeth.

When he rose again, he looked around at Layla. Then he turned to the assembled crowd in a solemn voice: "The god of the Christians has saved both our lives," he proclaimed.

To my ears, his words were eerily similar to those of the murdered apostle. He spoke unctuously and reverently.

I steered clear of Marcellus and the wolves that occupied the center of the room and hurried over to Layla. Apparently she had composed herself. She was just putting her woolen shawl around her shoulders and climbing out of bed.

I breathed a sigh of relief when I saw that she was unharmed.

"Did you hear it too, Thanar?" she asked me. "The voice that spoke to us?"

I nodded—and with difficulty resisted the impulse to pull her into my arms, where she would have found comfort and warmth.

"And you saw our savior, too? The fighter who slaughtered the wolves?"

Again I answered in the affirmative. I had recognized the outlines of a human-shaped figure and had seen a blade flashing in the silver light of the moon, so of that I was sure. The rescuer had been no more an illusion than the wolves were.

None of those present said a word. Morann snuggled even closer to Flamma. But even he—the glorious gladiator who had faced death so many times—looked smaller and lankier than usual, in the flickering light of the lamps.

Then, finally, the question I would have asked myself much earlier, had I been in my right mind, forced itself on me: How in the world had these beasts been able to invade my house? Had an evil demon conjured them up? They couldn't have just marched on their hairy paws right through my atrium! That was simply impossible. My doors were made of the best oaken timber. They were studded with iron. And to reach the bedroom of my friends, one had to cross the front part of the house first, past the slaves who slept not far from the main gate. Although, after the events of the past few nights, one could probably no longer count on their courage and vigilance. They must have been cowering in fear, like that fellow in the kitchen, huddling in one of the rooms and keeping their heads down when they heard the howling. Or the murderer had found a way to cast a spell on my household as well. With his intoxicating potion—or in an even more demonic way?

Severus detached himself from the wall he had been leaning against and limped toward Marcellus. He was still holding his head as if he were in great pain. I took a closer look at the wounds on his arms.

As if he had been bitten, went through my head—by beasts with sharp teeth. Beasts like those lying dead at our feet. Why hadn't I noticed this before?

"What happened to you?" asked Marcellus, who had also just now seemed to notice his centurion's stricken condition. The legate was staring at Severus, but his thoughts were clearly elsewhere. Still with that heavenly apparition that had just saved his life? And with the voice that had once again announced to him that he had been chosen?

The experience seemed to have made a deep impression on my friend. Marcellus was an ambitious man, vanity his Achilles heel. That the god of the Christians should have chosen him filled him with pride. One almost had the impression that he was basking in the glow of this new glory.

Severus, however, brought him back down to earth. "I was bludgeoned, legate," he cried accusingly. "Someone crept into my room and half bashed my skull in." As if to prove it, he took his hand from his temple and showed us the ugly laceration that gaped there.

"Bludgeoned, you say? Have not rather the wolves attacked you?" I asked sharply. I pointed to the wounds on his arms. They certainly hadn't been inflicted by a club or similar weapon.

Severus shook his head unwillingly. "I heard the beasts howling," he said. "They roused me from my sleep. But just as I was about to jump out of bed, someone hit me. I lost consciousness. That wasn't a wolf, for sure!"

"Could you recognize him then, your attacker?" asked Marcellus.

The centurion shook his head—and in the next moment pressed his hands against his temples again. He groaned and uttered a curse.

I sent a slave to get warm water and clean cloths. The centurion's wounds were not life-threatening, but they still needed to be taken care of.

XXXIII

I left the commotion behind. Marcellus would take care of Severus, and the dead wolves could do no more harm.

I had to know how the beasts had gotten into my house, because there were far more of them lurking out where they had come from, in the surrounding forests that seemed frozen in ice.

I rounded up my servants, had them light torches and sent them to check the doors, windows and walls of my house. I myself grabbed two lads and took the most direct route towards the main gate.

Already in the atrium I came across the trail of the beasts. Their paws had left wet spots—but there was more. Where the wolves had run along, there was also a clear trail of blood. Had one of the animals been injured even before they entered my house?

That seemed strange to me. A wounded wolf did not drag himself on the hunt with his pack. He would be nothing but a burden to the other beasts of his clan and thus a danger to their survival. No, an animal would not behave like this. Especially not a wolf.

When I reached the main gate, I found it closed. The heavy bolt, which secured it from the inside, had been pushed aside, however. That should not have been the case at this hour—but a wolf could hardly be responsible.

The floor here was also smeared with water and blood, and

the stench of wet wolf fur hung in the air. I could literally see before me how the beasts had run in here. In search of prey? Or what else could have lured them into my house?

The question remained how they had entered. I had expected to find one of the gates of my house broken open or damaged in some other way; possibly pushed in by the masses of snow, although that hardly seemed conceivable to me.

However, none of the slaves I had sent out to check on things returned to me with a report to that effect. No one had noticed a break-in.

"Someone must have let the wolves into the house," said a familiar voice at my back.

Layla.

She had probably followed without me noticing. Her fear seeming overcome, she stepped beside me and looked at the soiled floor. "Wolf paws, isn't it?" she said.

She bent down and picked up, without disgust, a small lump that looked like clotted blood. On closer inspection, however, it turned out to be the remnant of a piece of meat that had been torn to shreds by sharp teeth.

"Someone lured the animals here," Layla said. "It was the smell of fresh meat that made them invade your house." She rose and gestured with her hand toward the unbolted door. "Let's go check outside!"

I opened the gate before Layla could. The cold bit into my bare arms and calves. I wore nothing but the tunic I had hastily thrown on in my bedroom. Layla lowered her head and braced herself against the wind that was blowing toward us.

We didn't have to search long. In front of the house, my slaves—or Severus and his legionaries?—had taken up the fight against the masses of snow during the day. A narrow path, more like a ravine, led through the snow. As far as I could see, it extended to the stables and farm buildings.

Directly in front of the house gate, a small square area had been cleared as well as possible. Here the traces of numerous paws could easily be seen. They were quickly lost in the darkness, presumably leading over the man-high snowdrifts into the forest.

The snow had been no obstacle for the lightweight, four-footed beasts. They had run over it without sinking into it particularly deeply. And I also knew what had attracted them: Layla was proven right once again. For amidst the tangle of paw prints, there were also the footprints of a human being, and the remains of blood. They stood out bright red in the snow.

This time it was I who bent down and picked up some chunks of meat. Someone had crept out of the house in the middle of the night and prepared a royal meal for the wolves. First out here, to lure them out of the woods, then when they had tasted blood, there was more waiting for them inside.

The murderer—for I was sure that he was behind this new abomination—had opened the gate for the beasts and guided them through the house with a path of further scattered pieces of meat. The trail of blood I now followed with Layla ran from the main gate into the atrium, and from there straight on to Marcellus's room—through a narrow hallway that was otherwise little used. Especially at night time.

Now that I knew what I was looking for, the small scraps of flesh and the traces of blood were impossible to miss, even in the flickering light of the torches. The killer had made it a point not to encounter anyone if possible, but he had made no secret of his latest atrocity. *Wolves as a murder weapon.* Having already stabbed and poisoned ... what came next?

New hatred for this beast in human form took possession of me. This demon, beside which even the wolves seemed like innocent puppies, truly had to be in league with the darkest forces one could imagine.

Their greed for raw, bloody meat had led the wolves to exactly where the killer had wanted them. Arriving at the end of the bait trail, their hunger had been far from satisfied. In Marcellus's bedroom, they would have taken on the two sleeping humans—long before the legate would have had the chance to reach his sword and defend himself.

If this savior, supposedly sent by the god of the Christians, had not intervened so courageously, Marcellus and Layla would inevitably have been lost.

"Do you really think your legate could be ... could have been chosen?" I turned to Layla.

She raised an eyebrow and chewed her lower lip for a moment. "I don't know," she said then. "Who is able to fathom the will of the gods?"

She stood motionless for quite a while and seemed to ponder the question. "Marcellus is a great man, isn't he?" she finally said. "And we didn't hallucinate this savior. He was not a mirage. We all saw and heard him."

But why had the murderer chosen Marcellus as his latest

victim? Was he afraid that the legate would expose him and have him brought to justice? Or had the attack ultimately been aimed at Layla?

XXXIV

Just at that moment, I had an inspiration; a sudden clarity came over my mind. I felt as if I could finally escape the intoxicating influence of the kykeon potion.

"Severus!" escaped me abruptly.

Layla looked at me questioningly.

"I was just thinking about that story Severus told us. Don't you think it's a bit unbelievable? That he was attacked in his sleep, knocked out, and then injured in that peculiar way? Isn't it much more likely that the wounds on his arms came from the wolves—not because he got in their way, but because *he* let them into the house! The pieces of meat, with which he baited them, obviously had the desired effect. But what if the beasts thought their patron was a tasty meal as well, that they at least wanted to sample? What if they literally bit the hand that fed them?"

I looked at Layla expectantly, but she did not reply.

"Although I don't understand what motive could be driving Severus," I continued. "I mean, he is an exceedingly superstitious fellow and not very tolerant. He hates Christians and druids alike, I think. Maybe that's why he wanted them dead. But Marcellus? Why would he want to murder his legate? No, wait … yes, of course. That must be it! The Christian god seems to have chosen Marcellus as his new favorite, and the legate enjoys that distinction, doesn't he? For a man like Severus, it must amount to an unforgivable betrayal of the gods. Perhaps that's why he set the wolves on Marcellus. Yes, I think that's exactly how it must have happened! Don't you agree?"

I gasped for breath and was very pleased with myself for the moment.

Layla, however, remained silent. Only after a long while did I get an answer—which I found rather inappropriate. "We need to find out why Philomena had to die," she said, "I think her murder is the key."

"The key?" I repeated, uncomprehending. "Philomena?"

"The key that will explain the other crimes, the whole series of murders. If we understand why Philomena was killed, we'll get on the trail of the murderer, I'm sure of it!"

"Why Philomena of all people?" I asked.

"Because I can't think of any reason why she had to die. Paulus and Divicia were respected leaders of their cults—and they had enemies. Thessalos was a medicus, with expertise in poisons, wounds, and death. Perhaps this made him dangerous to the murderer in one way or another. But Philomena? She was nothing more than the wife of Paulus. I must confess that I first suspected her of being the killer, before she herself was stabbed. She was one of the few who had the opportunity to kill her husband and Divicia. She would have been able to poison Paulus with food or drink at dinner and then kill Divicia at the time when she supposedly found them both already dead. I had even figured out her motive for wanting to get rid of her husband; she didn't seem to me to be nearly as ardent a Christian as he was. I think she much preferred to be the wife of the argentarius than that of the apostle, who was ridiculed or even hated by everyone. She was a strong-willed woman and a conservative matron who placed a lot of importance on her reputation, and on a comfortable life."

"That all sounds plausible," I said, "it's just annoying that she was then killed herself. Or are you saying someone stabbed her because they knew she was the killer? Out of revenge? But then why set the wolves on Marcellus? None of this makes any sense."

Could Layla hear how frustrated I already was at this point? Instead of getting to the bottom of the original mystery—why Paulus and Divicia had been murdered—we were only getting more deeply entangled in new inconsistencies with each passing hour.

From one question, to which we had already found a halfway plausible answer, we were immediately confronted with three more, even more impossible ones. It was enough to make you jump out of your skin. I almost felt a longing to consume an entire cup of this kykeon substance and put an end to the unbearable chaos.

I received no answer from Layla. Behind her dark forehead her mind was working non-stop, you couldn't miss that. And I knew the look on her face when she was about to crack a seemingly unsolvable puzzle.

She looked exactly the same now. I felt like a complete fool next to her—but of course I didn't let it show.

I wish she'd let me in on her musings, but she would do that only once she had come to a satisfactory conclusion. That's how well I knew my black Sphinx.

But this time her theory did not make sense, I thought. The murder of Philomena was supposed to be the key? Surely

Layla had gotten onto the wrong track with that assumption.

Gently, I touched her arm to regain her attention. "Listen, Layla, you said earlier that Philomena was one of the few who'd had the opportunity to murder Paulus and Divicia. You're right about that; most of the others were able to prove their alibi to us. Only one could not—Severus. He was supposedly alone in his room while Thessalos chased after the imaginary griffin. And now he suddenly has wounds on his arms from an alleged attack. It was the wolves, I could swear! My money's on him, Layla! He's our killer!"

Again I received no answer. But I did not let myself be distracted by this anymore. "I will speak to Marcellus," I said, and immediately set about putting this plan into action.

I took the legate—and Layla—to my own room, where we could talk undisturbed. Like beggars, we feasted on nothing but water while I told Marcellus my suspicions.

I listed everything that told against Severus, and the legate listened to my explanations without interrupting me once. Layla remained silent as well—whether out of respect or because I had convinced her, I could not say.

When I had finished, Marcellus stared wordlessly into his long-emptied cup. Then he pushed it away from him and jumped up abruptly. "I'm going to talk to Severus," he said. "Alone."

XXXV

I didn't want to sit idly by while Marcellus cross-examined my main suspect. Besides, it was *the* opportunity to have a look around the centurion's room without having to fear that he would catch me.

Layla, of course, couldn't resist accompanying me, and so a few minutes later we were already busy rummaging through Severus' belongings, like thieves in the night.

He had hidden it well, but not well enough. In the end, I did discover it: a small glass vial with only a few drops of a pale gold liquid left in it. Severus had hidden it in the clothes chest between the folds of a tunic. So cleverly had the small vessel been tucked into the garment that a cursory examination would probably have left it undiscovered.

Triumphantly, I held it up and showed it to Layla. "How harmless it looks, don't you think? More like a love potion than a deadly intoxicant. But I'd bet the best horse in my stable that this is our demonic potion: kykeon. If the vial contained anything harmless, I'm sure Severus wouldn't have hidden it so well."

"Oh, I'm sure the liquid is kykeon," Layla said. Her tone sounded strange.

Again I got the impression that she was withholding a part of her thoughts from me, the essential part. She pulled the vial out of my hand and turned it between her fingers. She studied it with a critical eye.

She probably had to realize that I was on the right track, that the centurion was more than just suspicious.

"Let's get back to Marcellus," I said, taking the small jar back to myself. "I think he should know about this. I'm very curious to see how Severus is going to talk his way out now."

Just before I reached the legate's room, a slave came running toward me. "I'm glad I found you, master!" he cried breathlessly. "We have searched the whole house as you ordered. It's all safe, master. No one has broken in from the outside. The wolves could only have entered through the main gate. Someone must have opened it without authorization."

"Thanks, I figured as much."

"In the basement, however, we found one of the pantries looted," the slave continued. "Someone has tampered with the meat supplies, master."

I listened. It made all too much sense. The murderer—Severus, I was sure by now—must have used my meat to lure the wolves into the house. What exactly he had intended, I still did not understand. Had he really wanted to kill his legate in such a devious way?

Well, we would elicit the truth from him! And Marcellus would show no mercy. Four murders were a deadly outrage—but then to attack the legate personally? The worst of all punishments awaited the centurion. He would pay with an agonizing death, that much I already knew.

I thanked my slave, sent him away and hurriedly took the last few steps to Marcellus' room. Layla followed me silently like a shadow.

Through the closed door of the room came angry voices.

What was going on? It was not Marcellus and Severus who were having an argument here. The legate's commanding voice was clearly audible, but it was a woman's voice raised in reply.

XXXVI

I quickly opened the door and entered the room, together with Layla. I found it filled with a number of people for whom the space was barely sufficient.

It was Morann who was arguing with Marcellus. She stood in front of my friend like a goddess of vengeance. Small in stature as she was, she should have seemed like a child compared to Marcellus, but that was not the case. She was in a rage, and the legate seemed quite overwhelmed by her outburst.

To her right and left stood her two bodyguards, Granis and Cobanix, with their arms crossed in front of their chests. Their swords hung from their belts, clearly visible to all.

Behind Marcellus, however, Severus had taken up his position. His right hand rested on the pommel of his blade. In his weather-beaten face was an expression of the greatest disgust.

What had happened here? Hadn't Marcellus intended to grill his centurion as the main suspect, in a one-on-one conversation? Well, apparently nothing had come of it. The Celts must have burst into the room during this planned interrogation—and they made no indication that they wanted to leave soon.

"Thanar," Marcellus called out when he caught sight of me. He seemed very relieved to see me.

I stepped next to him to emphasize whose side I would

take should a fight break out in the next moment. It sure looked like it. I gazed into tense, hardened faces. Especially Morann, who had just spoken so hot-headedly, gave the impression that she wanted to pounce on the legate with claws and teeth in the next instant.

"I repeat it for the last time," she hissed. "We will not spend another night under this roof. And no one will stop us from leaving!"

Marcellus gave me an unnerved sideways glance. "Morann received a revelation from her gods," he explained to me, accompanying his words with a hand gesture that made it all too clear what he thought of this vision: not very much.

Morann immediately started to tell me what she had seen. "It is the god of these Christians who is behind the murders," she announced in the tone of a high priestess. "I already suspected it, already tried to warn you. But now the gods have given me certainty. You deluded fools! The one whom the Christians call their Lord and Father, before whom they throw themselves in the dust like slaves—he wants to make you believe that he is the highest, no, the only god. But in truth he is a dark demon! And the gate to the realm of the dead, which he pushed open, still stands ajar. More from our midst will die if we do not escape from this cursed place, as fast as our feet will carry us."

At that moment the door was pushed open. Flamma and Caecilia rushed into the room. The quarrel that Morann had started had certainly been audible in most of the house.

However, Flamma had apparently not overheard the words of Morann's revelation. As soon as he entered the room, he ran toward the druidess, pushed himself between the two Celts and wrapped his arms around her.

Caecilia didn't seem to want to put up with this any longer. "Stop, Flamma!" she shouted to her brother in the faith. "Let go of that witch! Do you not see how she has beguiled you, this dark succubus? She serves the forces of darkness!"

The two Celtic warriors jumped forward, ready to wield their swords—even if their opponent was an unarmed, weak woman.

Morann, however, raised her hand and stopped them.

Flamma stood motionless next to her, stiff and silent like a bronze statue. In his face, however, I read volumes. A battle was raging inside him—between the affection he so obviously felt for Morann, and his Christian faith, which the druidess had condemned in the most evil way.

"We have to leave this place," Morann repeated unperturbed. Her voice literally thundered through the room, something one would never have expected from such a delicate little person. "All of us, do you understand?" She stared first at Flamma, then at Marcellus, fixing—no, piercing—them with her gaze.

Marcellus groaned, but was unwilling to relent. "No one leaves this house until the murderer is exposed," he said. He spoke in a controlled tone, but with no less authority than the druidess.

"We should take Morann's warning seriously!" interjected Flamma. His words echoed through the small room as if he were wielding an iron hammer. "I will not tolerate another death!" He tightened his grip on Morann—a gesture that pleased neither the Celtic warriors nor Caecilia.

It was high time that I got involved. Those present had to

know what I had found out.

"You are mistaken, Morann," I said. "It is not the Christian god who has brought death among my guests, who has turned my house into a mausoleum. No, the murderer we seek is a man. And he dwells here among us!"

I had actually intended to present my evidence—the vial from Severus's chest—to Marcellus in private. But I would probably not get the opportunity again if I did not act now. At any moment, my guests could bash each other's heads in if I didn't intervene.

So I stepped forward and pulled the evidence from my pocket. "I found this—well hidden among your centurion's belongings," I said as I handed the vial to Marcellus. "I think he kept the poison in it with which he intoxicated us all. And with which he murdered Paulus."

A murmur went through the crowd. Everyone gathered around Marcellus to get a glimpse of the evidence.

"*He*, then!" the Celtic brothers shouted as if from one mouth—while Flamma only emitted an angry grunt. He seemed eager to go for the centurion's throat. By now, tempers were running so high that the slightest spark was enough to ignite an inferno. The men were ready to pounce on anyone presented to them as the guilty party and tear him to pieces on the spot. They would not bother with an investigation of the evidence or even the due process of law.

Severus reflexively took a step back, seeking protection behind his legate's back. That he could not take on these three men together was clear to everyone. "This is a slander," he cried angrily. "I am innocent!"

Marcellus silenced him with a commanding wave of his

hand. He gave the other men a look that could only mean one thing: *If you want him, you must first kill me. I am the one who decides right and wrong here.*

That cooled the tempers a little. But only for the time being, of that I was sure.

Marcellus looked at the vial I had handed him. "How do you know it contains kykeon, Thanar?" he asked.

"What else would it contain that Severus was so devious about hiding it?" I retorted.

Someone tugged at my sleeve. I was startled, wheeled around—and looked into the worried eyes of Layla. "I think you're making a mistake, master," she whispered to me.

I was not to know what she was trying to tell me, for Flamma pushed himself to the fore at that moment.

"Thanar is right, legate!" he shouted. "Leave Severus to me! This villain! This murderer! I'll beat the truth out of him yet."

The former gladiator was unrecognizable. Where had his Christian values gone? Peacefulness, charity? He seemed to have none of them for Severus.

"I had a talk with Severus," Marcellus took the floor again. "Just now, before we were … interrupted." He scowled at Morann and her warriors. "Severus swore to me on his honor that he had nothing to do with the murders. He was not attacked by the wolves, but knocked out in his bed. I—"

That was as far as he got. At that moment, Flamma exploded—and immediately infected the Celtic warriors with his wild rage. All previous hostilities between the three men suddenly seemed forgotten. Like old comrades in arms, they rushed together toward Severus, rudely jostling Marcellus aside. The legate—whom this attack caught unprepared—stumbled, lost his balance and went down.

Severus, however, reacted as quickly as a weasel. He ducked under Flamma's fist, which was aimed right at his face. He rammed his elbow into Granis' chest, making him gasp. Then he went down, but not because he was hit. Severus crawled a short distance on all fours—and all this at such a furious pace that I only realized what was happening when he had already reached the door. With this maneuver, he gave himself the tiny head start he needed to escape his captors. As if chased by the three Furies, he rushed out of the room.

The rest of us were in each other's way in the narrow chamber. I was rudely shoved aside by one of the Celtic warriors, then the two of them pushed out of the room. Flamma followed them. The three men took up the pursuit of the centurion.

Marcellus and I could only run after them like two lost strays.

XXXVII

In the hallway, Marcellus and I were able to close the distance to Flamma and the Celts to a few steps. With wild battle cries they pursued the fleeing centurion through the corridors of my house. I didn't get a good look at Severus himself, but he couldn't have had too much of a lead on his pursuers.

Outside, dawn was slowly breaking. Its dim light cast long shadows through the window panes and into the arcades of the courtyard we were crossing.

I had assumed that Severus would take the path through the atrium and then escape through the main gate. But the centurion chose a different route.

He seemed to know his way around my house. This was certainly not only due to the fact that he had dutifully performed his guard duty. If he was the murderer—on which I would have bet my right hand by now—he must have explored every nook and cranny, every narrow passage in my house, in order to go his way unobserved and to be able to carry out his misdeeds.

Severus's escape ended in one of the dining rooms, which was located on the south wall of my estate. This triclinium bordered on a terrace from which one enjoyed a magnificent view over the Danubius in the summer months. Now, of course, the terrace doors were locked against snow and cold. But Severus was already tampering with them when we caught up with his pursuers and pushed into the room to-gether.

The centurion rushed outside, out into the chest-high snowdrifts that were piling up on the terrace.

The cold hit us like a blow from a fist. It made us all stop for a moment.

I quickly turned around to check on Layla. Surely she had followed us as well. If she had been a typical woman, I would never have assumed that she would take part in the murder hunt. But Layla was everything but that.

I could not discover any trace of her, though. But I had no time to think about where she had gone. Severus's pursuers had already crossed the room and rushed out onto the ter-race with renewed battle-roars.

I saw the centurion struggling over the masses of snow like a four-legged predator, sinking in again and again.

The next moment he had reached the railing of the terrace, which was nothing more than a bulge in the unbroken white of the snow. I heard Severus gasp, saw him hesitate for just a tiny moment. In the next, he bravely pushed over this ob-stacle, which was hardly one at all—and let himself fall into the depths.

His pursuers climbed the railing and stared after him. Mar-cellus and I followed.

Below my terrace the terrain drops steeply, a good hun-dred feet down, until it reaches the bank of the Danubius. Such a leap as Severus had made would have been fatal in the summer. Now, however, the snow slowed his fall.

We saw Severus sliding down the slope in a swirling white cloud. He slid, skidded, rolled over several times, but got back to his feet at the bottom of the riverbank road, clearly unharmed. The road forms a narrow flat strip lining the river, but here, too, the snow was piling up.

Flamma and the Celts hesitated only for a moment. Then they did the same as the centurion, and dropped into the depths as well. They would not allow Severus to escape them by his daring maneuver. Snow flew up, then the men slid down the slope in white clouds, just as the hunted had done before.

"After them!" Marcellus cried, and before I knew what I was doing, we were both climbing the railing as well.

Breathless from the cold shock, mouth and nose full of snow, but otherwise unharmed, I landed behind the others on the shore road.

Where was the centurion going now? An escape in this weather, without coat or boots, with five pursuers at his heels? He had to know how hopeless it was. It could only be final desperation that still drove Severus, the certain knowledge that death awaited him if he did not at least try to escape.

For a moment he remained where he had landed, motionless on the spot. Only his head jerked first to the left, then to the right, like a predator that we had cornered and which was now desperately looking for an escape route.

I would have expected anything but the route Severus finally chose. Instead of fighting his way through the snow along the shore road, he headed straight toward the river.

It was an act of desperation—yet I understood in the next moment that the centurion had no other choice. The Danubius was covered with a layer of ice that had probably formed only the previous night. Only rarely did such low temperatures prevail in Vindobona that the mighty river froze over. Its waters normally rolled through the riverbed with such force that no ice could form. Now, however, it had happened—and since the ice layer was only a few hours old, it was not buried under the enormous mass of snow that had fallen in the last few days. Quite in contrast to the riverbank road.

When Severus ventured out onto the ice for the first few steps, he sank barely ankle-deep in snow.

Flamma and the Celts paused on the riverbank, half-submerged in the churned-up snowdrift in which they had landed. They were not sufficiently tired of living to follow the fleeing centurion out onto the river.

"Come, men, he must not escape us!" Fearlessly, Marcellus jumped into the breach Severus had made to reach the frozen waters.

"Hold on, legate!" I shouted after him. "You're running to your doom!"

Marcellus had already taken the first steps onto the ice—which apparently carried him safely, just as it also promised Severus free passage.

"Marcellus!" I screamed as loud as I could. The icy air burned like a potion of fire in my throat.

The legate came to a stop. He turned around with a jerk. "What's the matter with you? Are you going to let him escape? If he reaches the legionary camp, his soldiers will rally around him, all the men loyal to him. He will escape with their help—or even start a revolt in the camp!"

I did not doubt my friend's words. I understood why he

wanted to catch up with Severus at any cost. But Marcellus had only been stationed in Vindobona for a short time. He had not yet experienced how capricious the river god of the Danubius was. He had no way of knowing that the mirror-smooth surface of the ice, which glistened so invitingly in the sunshine and invited people to winter play, was in truth a deadly trap.

The ice may have looked frozen solid, but appearances were deceptive. Under the supposedly hard cover, the deeper waters of the river never came to rest. They pulled and tugged at the ice surface, creating tiny cracks that were barely visible to the human eye. And if a careless person ventured out onto the ice, it would break easily under his steps. In this way, the treacherous river god had already claimed numerous lives.

Severus had to know that, as he had served in Vindobona for many years. He had nevertheless chosen the way out onto the ice, but surely only because he saw in it his only hope, no matter how small it might be.

Marcellus, however, ran unsuspectingly toward his doom. He was probably deceived by the seemingly stable surface, which appeared even thicker because of the blanket of snow. Severus had already crossed the first third of the stream, and the legate now resumed his pursuit. He didn't seem to care that no one else had followed him.

I shouted after him from the shore several more times, implored him to turn around, screamed at the top of my lungs, but he couldn't—or wouldn't?—hear me.

Finally, I didn't know what to do. I briefly weighed up my options. *Let him go*, whispered a dark voice in the back of my head. *Then Layla would be yours again. Forever.*

I ignored this insidious impulse. Marcellus was my friend! I would have given anything to win Layla back, but I would not become a murderer because of her.

I mustered all my courage and ventured out onto the ice myself. At first I tentatively put one foot in front of the other, but I didn't make any progress that way. Marcellus was moving away from me faster and faster.

Finally, I abandoned all caution and rushed after my friend as fast as my feet would carry me.

"Marcellus," I cried, panting, "listen to me! The river will swallow you. You are running to your death. It's not worth it, stop!"

He came to an abrupt halt, right in the middle of the river. With a blush of anger on his face, he turned to me. "Damn you, Thanar!" he shouted. "He's going to get away from us!"

"He is doomed to die!" I cried. "And so are we if we don't finally turn back!"

I closed in on Marcellus, grabbed him firmly by the hand, and pulled him away with me, back toward the shore. Towards the safe embankment, away from Severus.

He cursed, but fortunately offered no more resistance.

The divine Danubius spared both our lives. The ice held. We reached the shore road, where Flamma and the Celts were waiting for us. They had not been willing to pay for the pursuit of the murderer with their own lives. Sensible men! No one could blame them.

I heard Flamma whisper an impulsive prayer to his god. "Lord, thank you for saving them."

At the top of the terrace, suddenly shouting and cheering

broke out.

I lifted my eyes—and saw that half a dozen of my slaves were crowding the terrace railing. They looked visibly relieved that Marcellus and I were unharmed. Two of them had brought thick ropes, which they now lowered to us. Strong lads stood ready to hoist us up, back into the protective warmth of my home. The two Roman legionaries had also taken up positions on the terrace. They, however, were not cheering. Their eyes were fixed on the river where their centurion continued his escape.

Marcellus and I did not yet rush to the ropes. Instead, we turned and stared after the fleeing killer.

Severus was running deftly across the ice. Three quarters of the distance to the salvation of the southern shore were already behind him. Had I been mistaken? Would he make it to shore unharmed? Was the capricious river god well-disposed toward this murderer?

Marcellus would never forgive me for that. In my mind, I could already hear him scolding me for being a pathetic coward, and breaking off our friendship. In the end, he would hold me accountable—whatever the centurion might have in mind as soon as he reached Vindobona.

My musings came to an abrupt end. When Severus accelerated his run once more to take the last steps towards the shore, it happened.

I heard the ice break even before I saw it. But then everything happened very quickly. Severus cried out and fell to the ground. The ice crunched, groaned, and in the next instant the horrified centurion sank into a frothing cloud of water, snow, and ice.

He briefly tried to save himself. He flailed his arms, cried for help, swallowed water, gasped.

With the strength of despair, he fought against his fate, which had long since been sealed. The floods of the Danubius embraced him in an ice-cold embrace and pulled him down to certain death.

XXXVIII

It was over.

At least that's what I thought, I the clueless fool. We who had hunted Severus stood on the bank, united in silence. As one man, we stared out at the river that had passed judgment on the fugitive murderer.

Let's go back to the house, I wanted to say. There was nothing more we could do here.

But before I could utter a word, music reached my ears: the delicate sounds of a lyre, which already seemed familiar to me, because I was not hearing them for the first time. Now they did not sound quite so unearthly as the last time, but it was certainly the same melody.

While I was still trying to locate where the sounds were coming from, a voice rose. It echoed over our heads, over the river, like the sound of a trumpet. And it was full of promise.

"Behold my power, I have judged the murderer! Kneel before me, mortals!"

At the top of my house a door burst open. It belonged to one of the exits that led out onto the terrace on the south side of my property. It was a good distance to the left of the one through which Severus had made his escape. I was sure that it had certainly not been open before.

"The god of the Christians, have you heard him?" Marcellus shouted in awe when the voice had faded away. He immediately obeyed the divine command and sank to his knees in the middle of the snow.

The next moment a white-robed figure appeared on the terrace. He climbed the snowdrift under which the railing was buried, got a secure footing on this elevation, then spread his arms in a solemn gesture.

I squinted my eyes. For a moment I thought I was watching another one of the visions that had nearly driven me out of my mind in the last days and nights. But I was no longer under the deceptive influence of the kykeon. I was freezing to the marrow of my bones, but my head was clear, my senses sharpened.

Up there, on the terrace of my house, stood Paulus—unharmed. Alive.

"I am the messenger of the Lord," the voice rose again, even louder and more insistent now. "I command death and life. Whoever follows me, no power on earth can harm him. Behold the miracle I have worked on my apostle!"

As if to emphasize these words, Paulus raised his arms above his head and stretched them toward heaven, his god, in a gesture of worship.

Without my wanting it, my knees gave way under me. Helplessly, I sank into the snow next to Marcellus. And yet I could not believe what I saw before me.

It is impossible, everything inside me screamed. My senses, my mind, even my boldest imagination revolted against the inconceivable. Paulus stood before me in the bright light of day. The man whose corpse I had seen with my own eyes.

Flamma literally threw himself to the ground, then the Celtic warriors also bowed their heads and finally knelt down as well, before the miracle that we had all witnessed. Before Paulus, whom his god had raised from the dead. He stood up there on the terrace, rejoicing, triumphant, like a symbol of blooming life. Not a vision, but a figure of flesh and blood.

"Behold, I—" the voice continued again, but the next moment a dull thud was heard—then an ominous silence spread.

Paulus flinched, turned, seemed to stare for a moment at something that lay behind him, hidden from our gaze. In the room to which this terrace belonged.

But the next moment the voice spoke to us again. "Behold, I will give you all another demonstration of my power. By commanding the elements!"

Was it just my imagination, or did the voice sound different? Loud and booming, it came down to us, as before, but it was deeper now, darker ... and I could have sworn that I knew it, as if it had already spoken to me a hundred times. At the same time it sounded strange and alluring, as if the vocal cords of the divine messenger were made of pure heavenly silver.

I pressed the heels of my hands against my temples. What was happening to me? Was it the proximity of this Christian god that confused me so?

"I am the Lord over wind and snow, cold and fire, water and ice," the voice continued. "Paulus, my faithful apostle shall walk where the heathen found no way. As once my son walked over the waters of the Sea of Galilee—so now Paulus shall walk over the frozen waters of the Danubius. You shall witness this miracle and praise my name. You shall obey my laws and proclaim the good news that I gave my only begotten Son—for your sins! Praise God, your Lord, and I promise you eternal life!"

I held my breath. Only then did I realize that I was still kneeling in the icy masses of snow on the shore road. I pulled myself up, stretched my neck to see better.

Out of the corner of my eye, I noticed that the other men were following my example. Marcellus, Flamma and the two Celts also rose—without taking their eyes off the reborn apostle for even a moment. The legionaries and my household, who had gathered on the other terrace, also stared as if spellbound at Paulus—through whom God was about to work another miracle. As if it was not enough that he had brought him back from the realm of the dead, from whence no one had ever returned!

Paulus himself, however, seemed scared to death at the new venture of his god. He did not seem at all eager to leave the safe terrace.

I could not understand his behavior. How could he be of so little faith? Wasn't he the most ardent apostle of the Christian god, and hadn't his Lord just raised him from the dead? What else could he fear? Should he not have the confidence to walk even over the burning coals in the hell forge of Hephaestus, if his God commanded him to do so?

"He is still weak, having just come back to life," said a voice beside me. Marcellus. There was a devout, nay, a completely rapt expression on his face. "Now come on, Paulus," he cried with fervor. "I will stand by you! Let us walk together across the river and enter Vindobona in triumph! I will have the most exalted temple built to your god, I swear by my life!"

He made the sign of the cross over his face with his thumb, in the way the Christians did.

XXXIX

Flamma joined in the shouts. He also swore his support to Paulus, vowing that he would protect him with his life until the end of time.

"Paulus, you ditherer! Do you want to oppose my will, when I have worked the miracle of resurrection on you?" the voice of the divine messenger thundered. A clear hint of anger now resonated in the words.

Paulus started to move. Hesitantly at first, but finally he dared to take the plunge. In a cloud of the finest powder snow, he glided down to us—exactly the same way we had reached the shore road ourselves.

Flamma was first on the scene to help him to his feet and hug him. "It's really you," he said. His voice sounded full of emotion and awe.

Marcellus did not miss the chance to embrace the resurrected apostle as well, and even the two Celtic warriors stared at him—from a safe distance—with a mixture of amazement and humility.

Paulus was shaking all over as he got to his feet.

"Do not be afraid, my son," the voice of the divine messenger came back. Full of majesty, it echoed over our heads.

The apostle looked back to my house once more, then tore himself away from the men who were supporting him and staggered toward the riverbank. Stiff and afraid, he took his first steps across the ice. He stopped, hesitated, and then took a route farther upstream than the one that had led the centurion to his doom.

Marcellus made an effort to accompany him. Flamma followed closely behind him.

"Stay back!" the divine command sounded. "Only on him will I work my miracle. You, my sons, must first prove yourselves worthy as he did. Watch and be in awe!"

Marcellus came to an abrupt halt. Deep disappointment spoke from his eyes as he looked back at me. He stood there indecisively for a moment, but finally returned to the shore.

Paulus, however, now seemed more undaunted. Almost at a run, he put one foot in front of the other, tracing a trail across the thin layer of snow that covered the ice. Watching spellbound, we followed his every step.

He reached the middle of the river unharmed. For a moment he slowed his run, bent over and seemed to struggle for breath. He gave us a look that seemed strangely empty and cold. Then he continued on his way.

Finally, he had completed three quarters of the way.

The voice of the divine messenger had fallen silent. Only the howling of the wind could be heard now. Paulus ran almost silently through the snow. Once he slipped, stumbled, but was able to catch himself with his arms and got back on his feet.

Finally, only a few steps separated him from the safe shore.

Then he had reached it. Marcellus and Flamma rejoiced, singing a song of praise in honor of their god, while Paulus sank down into the snow, exhausted—but certainly also relieved.

But then it happened. Branches cracked, snow fell from

the bushes and trees that grew along the riverbank. Suddenly, a dark shadow leapt out from between the branches—and lunged at the apostle.

A demon, was my first thought. But at second glance I realized that the attacker was a brown bear, one of those fearsome beasts that lived so numerously in the forests around Vindobona. The animal attacked with a bloodcurdling roar. No doubt it was as ravenous as the wolves that had invaded my house had been.

Paulus uttered a cry for help, stumbling to his feet, fleeing from the beast. But the masses of snow on the shore road hardly allowed him to move. The bear on its mighty paws was superior to him in every way.

The greedy roar of the beast made my blood freeze in my veins. I looked up to the sky, expecting at any moment that a thunderbolt would descend and strike down the beast. Surely the Christian god, who held his protective hand over Paulus, would save him from death again.

But nothing happened.

"We have to save him," a man's voice yelled right next to me. Marcellus. He ran, jumped down again onto the ice of the Danubius, unsheathed his sword, and charged across the river.

"Stop, legate!" shouted the voice of the divine messenger, which all at once echoed across the river again.

But this time my friend paid it no attention. All his thinking and striving seemed to be for Paulus only. Marcellus was one of the bravest fighters I knew, and a man who was willing to risk his life to protect a friend. I had seen him fight a bear once before—a duel to the death, in which the beast had lost out in the end. But would he reach Paulus in time before the beast mauled the defenseless man?

Then another, even more urgent, question tormented me: Would the ice carry Marcellus as it had carried the apostle?

"Marcellus!" the voice called again. But it was no longer the same. Something had changed. It sounded even louder than before, as if a woman was screaming at the top of her lungs.

Yes, that was it, a woman! But not just any woman. This voice clearly belonged to Layla! Her echoing sound was gone all at once.

I wheeled around, stared up at the terrace—and there she stood. Layla. She was kneeling on the snow-covered railing. "Marcellus!" she cried at the top of her lungs. "Hear me! Turn back. You can't save him!"

The legate also seemed to have noticed the change now, that the messenger of the Lord suddenly spoke to us in Layla's voice. He came to a skidding halt, looked around, and recognized Layla without a doubt, for he had the keen eyes of youth.

Just at that moment, Paulus uttered his last cry. The bear had caught up with him. Roaring wildly, the giant animal reared up above its victim. It bared its teeth—then it struck. Nothing or no one could save the apostle now.

"Marcellus!" shouted Layla again. "Come back, I can explain everything!"

Marcellus hesitated. Surely he did not understand how the messenger of the Lord had suddenly turned into Layla any more than I did. But he had to realize that he could no longer help Paulus.

I felt dizzy. Gasping, I went down on my knees, closed my

eyes, and fought off the nausea that was taking hold of my guts.

When I looked up again, Marcellus had started on his way back. Uncertainly he ran toward me, across the river, which could still swallow him.

Please let the ice carry him, I prayed—without knowing to which god I should now direct my plea.

On the south bank of the Danubius, the snow had turned blood red—while the bear was gorging itself on its prey.

XL

The strongest of my slaves helped us find our way back into the house. With the help of the ropes they had brought, they hoisted us up to the terrace. Without this support we would never have been able to climb the embankment—even if the way down had been easy.

Of course, there might have been other ways back. But this was the most immediate and the fastest. To get to the other entrances to my house, we would first have had to laboriously make our way through snowy embankments that buried everything underneath them.

I expected to find Layla among the men who met us on the terrace. I couldn't wait to hear her explanation for the incomprehensible happenings I had just witnessed. But she was nowhere to be seen.

I cleared my way, ungently pushing aside the well-meaning souls who wanted to wrap me in warming blankets. I would express my gratitude to them later. Hastily I crossed the room that lay behind the terrace. I ran along the corridor, on the direct way to that chamber on whose terrace the resurrected apostle had appeared. That was where I had last seen Layla—when she had revealed herself to Marcellus.

The legate followed me. So did the other men, judging by the multitude of footsteps that were echoing at my back.

When I reached the door of the chamber in question, I pushed it open without pausing even for a moment.

And there she was: Layla.

She was standing right in front of me, in the middle of the room. In one hand she held a silver amphora, like the ones I used to serve my best wines, and in the other … a dagger? And Layla was not alone in the room. In a corner, to the right of the terrace doors, a woman was crouching. She looked dazed and completely frightened.

Caecilia.

I no longer understood anything at all.

Marcellus seemed to be faring no better. He rushed toward Layla, but stopped abruptly when he saw how strangely armed she was.

"By Jupiter," he snapped, "what's going on?"

Layla seemed infinitely relieved to see us. Suddenly she pressed the dagger and the amphora into my hands, while all tension seemed to disappear from her body. Exhaling deeply, she dropped onto one of the two sofas that were part of the room's furnishings.

"I thank the gods for bringing you back to me unharmed," she whispered, closing her eyes for a moment.

I was beginning to think she was going to faint—but not Layla.

Some slaves appeared in the doorway. When Layla caught sight of the lads, a grateful smile flitted across her lips. She looked at Marcellus, then at me. Concern for our welfare was in her dark eyes.

"I can explain everything to you," she said. As she did so, she cast a meaningful sideways glance at Caecilia, who was pressing herself against the wall, whimpering. "But first you should put on dry clothes and warm up a bit. You must be half frozen!"

My servants did not wait for my instructions first; Layla's word seemed to be just as valid to them. One after the other they scurried out of the room, to return immediately with fresh clothes and the warm blankets they had already offered.

Another fellow supplied a small brazier to quickly heat the room. The last brought two amphorae of wine and a tray full of drinking cups. The wine vessels were still sealed, thus I harbored no concern that we would again poison ourselves with some potion. I willingly had a cup filled. I drank the wine undiluted, as only barbarians used to do, but I didn't care at that moment. The strong brew burned pleasantly down my throat and awakened my spirits.

Caecilia, meanwhile, regained her speech. She pulled herself up, but then pressed herself again against the wall at her back. As if the solid masonry could give her protection. "That madwoman tried to kill me!" she cried, pointing an accusing finger at Layla.

My Nubian, however, was unimpressed. She did not even dignify the Christian with a glance.

I could no longer stand the tension. "Tell us what happened, dear," I cried—before I realized that I shouldn't call her by that term of endearment in the presence of Marcellus.

"Severus was not a murderer," Layla began abruptly. She knew how not to beat around the bush, but to astonish her listeners with her very first words. You had to give her that.

"Not a murderer?" said Marcellus. He had settled on the sofa right next to Layla, while I had taken a seat on the opposite bench. Flamma sat next to me, and the two Celts leaned against the wall behind us. We were all surrounded by my slaves, who had to be as eager for answers as I was. I did not have the heart to send them away.

Would Layla be able to clear up everything we had experienced in the last few hours? Was that even possible? Nothing made sense to me anymore.

She, however, who had also wrapped herself in a warming blanket, now spoke calmly and deliberately, as if weighing her every word carefully. "Your centurion was slandered," she said to Marcellus. "He died without guilt."

All at once I remembered the words Layla had whispered to me—earlier, in Marcellus' room, when we had put the centurion through the wringer, just before he had fled—*I think you're making a mistake, master.*

But I had not listened to her. I had been so eager to finally hunt down the murderer that I had paid no attention to her quiet protest.

A vague feeling of remorse spread through my heart. Was Layla speaking the truth? Had Severus really been innocent?

"You all went after Severus," Layla continued, "but we women stayed behind. As befits the female folk, doesn't it?" She gave Caecilia a fleeting glance. "I pretended to retire to my room to recover a little from the terrible commotion. But in truth I did nothing of the sort. Rather, I took the opportunity to follow Caecilia like a silent shadow. I wanted to see where her way would lead her. And what did I find? She disappeared into the Christian prayer room and stayed there for quite a while. Did she just want to devote herself to a meditation? No. It was worth my while to lie in wait. Soon she left the room again—in the company of the man who had been laid out there as dead. Paulus! "

"His god raised him from the dead," Marcellus said—although after all that had happened, he didn't seem to quite trust his own words. A deep wrinkle had appeared on his youthful forehead. He no longer spoke in the tone of complete conviction that he usually so readily displayed, but instead rather timidly.

"No, legate," Layla contradicted him. "His god could not have raised him from the dead at all. Because Paulus was never dead to begin with!"

XLI

It was as if Layla had hurled Jupiter's divine lightning bolts right into our faces.

"*Never dead?*" I repeated, uncomprehending. Had she lost her mind?

"Now listen," Marcellus also protested. "He may not have been stabbed, as we assumed at first, but he was undoubtedly murdered. With poison, this kykeon, wasn't he? We all saw his body, after all."

"We saw it," Layla said, "but we didn't examine it in detail. We wanted to leave that to the medicus—but he never got around to it."

She paused. Then she said, "This is exactly why Thessalos had to die; because he would certainly have noticed that Paulus was still alive during the planned examination."

She fixed her dark eyes on me. "When you and I found Paulus poisoned yesterday morning, he must have been near death. His life may have been hanging by a thin thread, for he was indeed poisoned. But the dose was wrongly measured, by the murderess who wanted his death. The amount was not enough to kill him. It merely caused him to sink into a death-like sleep."

"But we should have noticed that," I protested.

Layla gave me a thoughtful look. "Really? As I said, we didn't look closely, because we simply assumed that Paulus was dead. We didn't check to see if his heart was still beating, and even if it was, we might not have noticed. Doesn't it happen very often that people are buried alive? It is not easy to recognize death for sure. Many a supposedly deceased person has found himself alive in his tomb."

"Murderess, you said?" Marcellus interjected. "A *woman*?" My friend sounded as perplexed as I was.

"Maybe I should start at the beginning," Layla said. "I'll try to tell you about my musings over the last few days, and how they led me to the truth in the end."

"Excellent idea," Marcellus grumbled. "I'd like to finally know who murdered whom here. And above all, why! Otherwise I'll lose my mind!"

A suggestion that I could only confirm. At least I was not the only one who seemed to be completely in the dark. A small consolation!

For a moment, a mischievous smile played around Layla's lips. She seemed to be very sure of herself. And she was clearly enjoying the triumph of being the only one to have solved the murder case.

The next moment she spoke to us again in her usual modest and calm manner, as if she were giving us a purely factual report—not another testimony to her amazing ability to get at the truth. To solve impossible mysteries, to hunt down murderers who thought they were smarter than everyone else.

"It's not easy at all to find the beginning in this terribly tangled business," she mused. "We were so blinded by all the daydreams, visions, and mirages that haunted our every step. Each of us saw something different. Things we desired, beings we feared, people we'd lost.... Only on two occasions did several of us see and hear the same thing. So this could not have been a mirage of our senses, I thought to myself. Both times it was the voice that spoke to Marcellus."

"The divine messenger," the legate confirmed with a nod of his head.

Layla raised an eyebrow, which was in keeping with her polite way of letting Marcellus know he was wrong, without contradicting him directly in front of everyone gathered.

"At first, I actually thought this apparition was a messenger from the Christian god," she said, "and it made sense to me that this Almighty would choose you as his new adept. After all, you're not just very influential in Vindobona, but you come from a distinguished family, you're an outstanding commander and leader, and you're bound to go far in the Empire."

Layla gave the legate a look full of tender pride. "Marcellus could make a difference for this Christian god," she continued, addressing the rest of us. "He could bring him recognition, perhaps even renown, in our province and beyond. But what I didn't understand was why this God sent a heavenly warrior to save Marcellus from the wolves—when he couldn't save Paulus from the bear? Or didn't want to?"

That was a legitimate question. Why hadn't I asked it myself?

"If I can't understand something," Layla continued, "if an explanation seems nonsensical to me, I try to go through every conceivable possibility. As for this purported messenger of god who protected Marcellus but left Paulus to die, there were only two alternative explanations: first, he—and by extension, the god who sent him—were in fact demonic beings. Dark creatures who do not care whether a person lives or dies. But why should such a demon have pretended to Marcellus to be the Christian god? Marcellus had—at least at the beginning—no preference for Christianity. Wouldn't it have been easier for a demon to pretend to be Jupiter, Apollo, or any other of the known gods if he wanted to win Marcellus over?"

"I think so," I agreed with her, even though I didn't yet understand what she was getting at.

"Possibility two: if the alleged Christian god who seemed to be so interested in Marcellus possessed neither divine nor demon nature, he could only be a man, and one who had merely *pretended* to be a divine messenger. This possibility seemed to me the most probable, even if the voice that spoke to us had a heavenly sound. Strictly speaking, we had to deal with *two* people. Because the figure that killed the wolves with their sword was not the same one that spoke to us. The angelic voice we heard seemed to come through the walls of the room. It did not emanate from the savior who wielded the sword."

Now it was Marcellus who raised his eyebrows skeptically.

Layla, meanwhile, continued to speak unperturbed. "But who would want to fool Marcellus into believing in the god of the Christians, I wondered. Only an ardent Christian, right?"

"Paulus," I said, without hesitation. "He wanted to spread Christianity, and Marcellus would have been very useful to him, with his power and influence, as you have just described it. But Paulus was dead, after all." I still didn't understand how the apostle had suddenly appeared on the terrace alive and kicking. Would Layla be able to explain this miracle to us?

XLII

Marcellus was visibly uncomfortable with Layla's revelations. I knew that he had taken the proclamations of the supposed divine messenger at face value. He had basked in his vanity, in being the chosen one of a god.

"It was not a human voice speaking to us, Layla," he objected. "You heard it yourself."

Layla got up from the sofa and walked over to the silver amphora she had been holding earlier. Now the vessel stood on the floor near the door. Layla lifted it up, to just below her lips. She spoke into the vessel in a loud and solemn voice: "There are many ways and means to distort one's voice, Marcellus," she proclaimed—suddenly sounding an awful lot like the messenger of a god. The metal of the amphora gave her voice that unearthly reverberation that had impressed us so much.

The legate expelled his breath, startled. "Damn it," he snapped. "How could I have fallen for that?"

"If you had been master of your senses, this would hardly have been possible," Layla said. "The kykeon that intoxicated all of us made it impossible for us to distinguish illusion from reality. That's exactly why it was administered to us, I think. To blind our senses to what was really happening in the house, while at the same time making us more susceptible to those things we were being led to believe. Like this supposed messenger of the gods."

Marcellus gave me an embarrassed look. I knew exactly what was going on in his mind; I also felt like the biggest fool.

"So I suspected there must be two conspirators," Layla said, "who belonged to the Christian camp. Paulus was dead, at least that's what I believed. So only Flamma, Caecilia and Philomena came to mind. My first guess was Philomena. Who could be her assistant, I did not yet know enough to say. Maybe all three of them were in cahoots? But then Philomena herself was stabbed, at the same time as the medicus, which made no sense at all. I couldn't get any further with my thoughts as long as we were all under the influence of the kykeon. If I hadn't been so infatuated and confused, I might have been able to save Severus."

Her voice died to a whisper. "We drove him to his death, although he was completely innocent. He merely fled from us because he was afraid of being torn to pieces the next moment. He had no chance to defend himself."

Layla let her gaze wander around. To Flamma, to the Celts. None of the men said a word.

She continued, "When you were chasing after Severus, I took the opportunity to sneak after Caecilia, as I have already reported. She was the only one of the Christians left in the house. She and Flamma were the only two still alive. So I strongly suspected her of being behind the pretended messages from her god, and thus the murders. But I could not prove anything. Then, however, when she left the prayer room with Paulus, who was alive and unharmed, everything became clear to me. It was he who had committed the murders, and she had been his accomplice!"

Layla looked around once again. Perhaps she expected to meet with opposition. But no one had anything to say.

She continued with her accusation: "Paulus had been the one who let the wolves into the house—and he also slipped into the role of the divine knight who saved Marcellus and me from the beasts, while Caecilia played a little melody in the adjoining room. In our intoxication we thought we heard heavenly sounds. She used a lyre to make her music. See, the instrument is over there in the corner. She also spoke into the silver amphora in a raised voice, and we were all fooled by it."

She paused, seeming to lose herself in thought.

"Keep talking," Marcellus urged. "What happened then?" He was scowling, but at the same time seemed highly impatient to finally know the whole truth.

Layla nodded her head and did as she was told. "I sneaked up behind the two of them after they left the prayer room and followed them here to this room. It was fortunately still dark in the house, so I made it behind the sofa unnoticed and was able to hide. Caecilia left once more and then returned with the amphora and the lyre. Then she blocked the door from the inside, with the little wooden wedge there, see? While Paulus opened the terrace door a tiny crack and peered out. For quite a while he remained at this observation post. I assumed he was following how you chased Severus. Then, however, he suddenly gave a hand signal to Caecilia, who was standing close behind him. She picked up the lyre, and played a little tune. Next she grabbed the amphora, while Paulus pushed open the terrace door all the way. He stepped out, and she began to speak in the name of her god—amplified by the metal body of the amphora. Then one thing became clear to me: if the voice of the divine messenger was nothing but a trick, could the raising of Paulus from the dead be genuine? Absolutely not! So the only conclusion that remained was that he had never been dead."

At this point I understood what must have happened next. "The voice stopped all of a sudden," I said to Layla. "Right after that, we heard a kind of thud. A dull sound, as if something heavy had fallen to the ground. And after that, the divine words sounded changed. The voice suddenly seemed strangely familiar. Oh, I am an old fool. It was you, Layla, wasn't it? You knocked Caecilia down and took her place! What did you do to make her go down? Snuck up behind her, snatched the amphora from her, and then hit her on the head with it?"

Layla smiled sheepishly. "I guess that's how it happened, master. I had no choice. I had armed myself with a dagger, but there were two opponents. I would have had to round up some slaves or the legionaries first, but then the two conspirators might have noticed me. After that, they would certainly not have been caught a second time red-handed in their pretty little performance. And who would have believed me then, that it was not the Christian god himself who had resurrected Paulus and let his messenger speak to us? So I was on my own. I put Caecilia out of action and took her role. Then I had to think of something very quickly."

"The divine miracle of Paulus," I said. "That he should walk across the water and reach the other shore unharmed, while Severus had gone under." I would never have thought of such an idea in so short a time.

Layla nodded. "Paulus, of course, noticed that it was no longer Caecilia who was speaking to you. He turned to me. *You are a murderer,* I whispered to him. I didn't have time for long explanations, threats, or even for proof. I showed him my dagger—and he obviously trusted me to make use of it if he attacked me. *Let the gods decide whether you should live or die,* I said to him—then I continued speaking to you, forcing him to take flight. He had a real chance of making it across the river alive and then going into hiding somewhere. Even if it was a small chance."

"Paulus took it," I said.

"Yes. He must have realized that he had no alternative. After a brief moment of hesitation, he obeyed what appeared to be a divine command. Perhaps he still thought that his god would save him. Presumably, after all, he believed he was acting on divine orders when he became an assassin, when he decided that Divicia had to die. The pagan who worshipped what were demons in his eyes, and who now wanted to capture the Empire for her cult, with her magic remedy against the plague. She promised a greater miracle than he or any other Christian apostle had ever worked with the help of his god. This could not be allowed to happen! Rather, Paulus wanted to win the world to his faith."

"That's why he came up with the idea of his own resurrection?" I interjected. "The greatest of all miracles."

"I think so," Layla said. "He decided to kill Divicia and at the same time demonstrate the power of the Christian god over life and death. That's why he made himself a murder victim as well—only ostensibly, of course. The resurrection was part of his plan from the beginning. Just like the ruse with the divine voice, which he devised to additionally win Marcellus as an intercessor, nay, as a new believer."

"But in the end, I guess his god let him down," I said. "Instead of saving him, he sent him a bear."

Layla nodded wordlessly.

XLIII

"How Paulus faked his own murder—you'll have to explain that to me," Marcellus demanded. "So he is supposed to have killed Divicia. Well, I can imagine that. He wanted to prevent her from succeeding with her plague remedy and possibly winning the Emperor's favor, while the Christians reaped laughter for their faith at best. At worst, they would face hatred, persecution and death. I assume he stabbed Divicia after she took him to her room for a friendly chat?"

"That's how it must have happened," Layla said. "He pretended to get over his initial hostility toward her, and instead cozied up to her all day long, so he could get a chance to be alone with her without arousing suspicion."

Layla turned to me, "Do you remember, Thanar, what one of your slaves claimed? He swore that he had been keeping an eye on the hallway outside Divicia's chamber all evening. And that no one had entered the room."

He had been right about this, I now had to admit to myself, even if the superstitious fellow had drawn the wrong conclusion from his observation. No supernatural being had crept unseen into the chamber and become a murderer there; Paulus, who had been in the room all the time, had committed the bloody deed.

"Probably Paulus got the druidess to show him the plague medicine first," Layla said. "Then he killed her and destroyed it. He stained his own robe with her blood and inflicted a few cuts on his arms with the dagger. He must also have applied these pretended defensive wounds on Divicia when she was already dying. There was no long fight between the two, otherwise Divicia would surely have screamed for help. He inflicted these wounds on her—and himself—to make the fight scene more believable. Everyone should immediately jump to the conclusion that two people had been stabbed here."

"And then?" asked Marcellus.

"Philomena must have been in on it, as was Caecilia. Only Flamma was clueless, I think."

"Completely clueless!" affirmed the former gladiator. "I can't believe that behind my back such an intrigue—"

He broke off abruptly and shook his head unwillingly. When he looked over at Caecilia, she merely stared stubbornly at the floor in front of her, as if the accusation were none of her business.

Layla continued, "I think that's what the argument between the three of them was about, in the run-up to the murders. Paulus presented his deadly plan to the two women. He implored them to support him in it—which they rebelled violently against at first. Understandably so. But finally he convinced them, perhaps with the argument that his god had personally ordered him to commit the murder and to stage the resurrection miracle? I don't know, but it doesn't matter. In any case, Paulus agreed with his two accomplices that they would 'find' him in Divicia's room, apparently stabbed as well. The room was in semi-darkness when Philomena raised the alarm and we all showed up there. She and Caecilia gathered around the supposedly murdered apostle, crying—which kept us from having the idea to subject the body to a thorough examination right there and then. No one wanted to be so tactless as to disturb the mourners in their grief."

"But what became of the dagger with which Paulus committed the bloody deed?" I asked. "We didn't find it anywhere in the room."

"I suspect he hid it under his own body," Layla said, "where of course no one was looking for it."

I admired how she immediately had an answer ready to every objection, every question. She must have thought through the murderous mystery—and its solution—down to the smallest detail, and in such a short time.

But Marcellus was already asking her the next question: "But how did it happen that we found Paulus poisoned the next morning? He didn't fake that as well, did he? You spoke of an assassin. And that he only narrowly escaped death."

Layla nodded thoughtfully. "One of his allies had her own plans for him. She realized that the spectacle Paulus staged around his apparent murder presented her with a unique opportunity. Paulus was going to be resurrected to demonstrate to the world a miracle of his god, but she was planning to get rid of her husband—who was no longer the one she had once married."

"You mean ... Philomena?" I asked incredulously.

"Oh yes, and she used his own poison to do it: the kykeon, with which he drove us all out of our minds. She gave him a strong dose of it, during the night when he was playing dead, his apparent corpse having been laid out in the prayer room. She poisoned him when she supplied him with fresh drinking water, I suppose. She made the mistake, however, of measuring too little of the poison. When Caecilia checked on Paulus early in the morning, she thought he was dead, just as we did. But he was merely walking on the banks of the river of death."

Layla paused for a moment, then asked me, "Do you remember the jar that Caecilia dropped, Thanar? The smell of its contents made you think of a latrine. I was wrong to believe that she had come into the room with it to perform some Christian ritual. She wanted to *remove* the jar from the room. To empty it inconspicuously."

I didn't immediately understand what Layla was getting at—but the next moment the scales fell from my eyes. "The jar contained exactly what you normally smell in a latrine, didn't it?" I exclaimed. "Urine! Paulus was playing dead, you say. He lay under the shroud in the prayer room. That was his hiding place, so to speak, where he would have held out for a few days and then miraculously risen from the dead. He could do without food for this time, but not without water—and thus he also had to empty his bladder occasionally. It was the task of his two helpers to take care of his needs. Philomena took over the night watch and brought him water when we were all asleep. Caecilia, early in the morning, wanted to take the telltale amphora away that Paulus had used as a chamber pot. In doing so, she found him apparently dead. She immediately concluded that Philomena must have poisoned him, for only she, as a co-conspirator, had known that Paulus was still alive. And she had had the opportunity that night to poison her husband, who, with his new faith, had made a mockery of her and forced upon her a life she detested."

The words just bubbled out of my mouth. My mind suddenly seemed lively. Now that I was listening to Layla's explanations, the terrible events suddenly didn't seem so inexplicable to me.

She nodded at me appreciatively and took the floor again. "When we interrogated Caecilia shortly afterwards, she directed our suspicions to Philomena. Remember? She did it in a very subtle way. On the one hand, she informed us that Paulus's wife always prepared his drink and food. And that she had probably preferred being the argentarius's wife to her new existence as a Christian. At the same time, however, Caecilia repeatedly emphasized that Philomena would never harm her husband after all. So she didn't accuse her directly, but she still made us suspect Philomena. Very clever indeed."

Layla looked over at Caecilia, but she still showed no reaction. She seemed to have taken refuge in a state of inner prayer. Her lips barely moved, her eyes seeming to look into another world that lay far beyond ours.

"Paulus must have also realized who was trying to poison him," I built on Layla's explanations. "After he survived the attack and regained consciousness. When we left him yesterday morning, he was close to death, but in the hours afterward he must have regained his strength. And then he realized what had happened, that his own wife, who had supplied him with water the previous night, had mixed poison into his jug. Full of anger, he decided that she deserved to die. That treacherous traitor! He took the dagger that was still in his possession and sneaked into Philomena's room, which was right next to the prayer room, so the risk of being seen during this excursion was small. After committing the deed, he returned to lie under his shroud and played the dead man again."

"This must be how it happened," Layla confirmed.

"And Thessalos?" I continued. "He probably decided to check on the dead in the early evening hours, when he had some of his strength back. Didn't he? He wanted to give the bodies a closer examination, as was natural for a medicus. I imagine that he went to the prayer room where Paulus should have been laid out—and found him not dead at all? Had Paulus just returned from killing his wife? Or was he lying under his shroud—knowing full well that he would not be able to play dead under the critical gaze of the medicus? In any case, Thessalos had to die as well."

"And what about me?" Marcellus took the floor. "Why did he set the wolves on me?"

"He didn't want to kill you, legate," Layla said. "Up until this point, he had been using poison and the blade, so why suddenly rely on wolves now? That's an extremely awkward and unsafe way to kill someone, isn't it? No, the wolves served only one purpose: he wanted you to witness a miracle. He made you believe that the Christian god had sent a heavenly warrior to save you. He played this role himself, while Caecilia took over the divine voice. As I said before, Paulus wanted you to become a powerful advocate for Christianity."

"Besides, the attack of the wolves was an opportunity to cast suspicion on Severus," I said. "Your centurion should pay for the murders. Presumably Caecilia overheard us discussing him as the prime suspect. She reported this to Paulus, and they both found that he made an excellent culprit. He tended to have a temper, and he hated both the Christians and the Celts equally. So they hid the kykeon vial in his room—where we promptly found it."

"They hid it well enough that it didn't look planted, yet poorly enough that we would find it," Layla said. "And Severus spoke the truth when he claimed to have been attacked in his bedroom. Paulus knocked him out, presumably just before he let the wolves into the house. He made the wounds on his arms look like bites or claw marks—"

"And we promptly fell into his trap," I concluded bitterly. "Severus paid for our blindness with his life!"

XLIV

Marcellus gave me a gloomy look. He probably hated himself just as much as I in turn despised myself.

"You," he turned in a gruff voice to Caecilia, who was still cowering on the floor, "get up and come here. I have questions for you!"

The Christian woman rose as if she had aged thirty years. With a crooked back and a shuffling gait, she stepped in front of the legate. She did not dare to look him in the eye.

"Tell me, woman, do you confess yourself guilty?" asked Marcellus in a cutting tone. At the same time he fixed Caecilia with his dark eyes, as if he were already crucifying her, as was a popular punishment for murderers. "Did you commit all these atrocities together with Paulus? Did it take place as we have heard?"

"Yes, lord," Caecilia replied. Her voice was no more than a dry whisper.

"What poison have you given us, to beguile us? To make us see miracles and demons, and to make us susceptible to your cunning deceptions? Was it kykeon?"

The Christian nodded, barely noticeably.

"Answer me when I ask you a question," thundered Marcellus.

Caecilia opened her eyes in shock. "Yes, lord, it was kykeon. Paulus mixed a small amount of it into the wine amphorae and into some of the food. We ourselves drank only water since the evening when ... when everything began."

"And you were the so-called messenger of god, who spoke to us?"

"That is also true, lord. But don't you see that Paulus only wanted to open the eyes of all of you with his deeds?" she added. Her voice gained strength. "The people of our corrupt age are stricken with blindness and deafness. They worship false idols and demons. They do not hear God's voice, and misjudge His signs! We have only helped a little to lead you to the Lord. I served God as a mouthpiece. But I only did and said what he told me to do. Do you truly think you could bear the sight of a real messenger of heaven? The angels of God are of such glory that we would go blind at the sight of them. Or worse!"

Caecilia now raised her head. Speaking of her faith seemed to give her new courage. "It was God Himself who revealed the secret of the kykeon to Paulus," she explained. "In his travels, when he was still the argentarius, he came across an adept of the Eleusinian Mysteries—who told him the secret of the brew and its ingredients. Paulus drank of it, but in holy intoxication he did not see the false gods of the Greeks! He met Christ, our Lord. The pagans abuse the Holy Plants for their depraved orgies. But those who are pure in heart find the way to the true, the only God with these herbs. Paulus worked many miracles with the help of the potion. He healed people with it. He cast out demons. And God spoke to him and told him to preach the good news, everywhere in the Empire, wherever he went. Jesus Christ was with him at all times."

"Then I suppose this god also guided Paulus's hand when

he became a murderer?" Marcellus interposed. "Don't you realize what nonsense you are talking, woman?"

But Caecilia was not deterred. "We are all damned if God does not save us," she cried with fervor. "Paulus wanted to show people the right way—which is worth any sacrifice! It was God's will that we should come upon this witch here in Thanar's house. She wanted to seduce you, Marcellus, with her dark magic. We could not stand idly by! The Empire must find the true faith—instead of being taken over by a druidic witch. We destroyed her demonic magic powder and silenced her forever!"

Caecilia now had her arms folded in front of her chest. She stood upright, almost defiantly, in front of Marcellus and jutted out her chin.

My friend turned around, addressing his two legionaries. "Get her out of my sight," he ordered, "and put her in shackles. When we get back to camp, I will decide her fate. But do not count on my mercy, woman," he turned back to Caecilia.

"Only God can judge me," she replied—and spat at Marcellus' feet. But then she let the two soldiers lead her out of the room without resistance.

XLV

Marcellus didn't want to spend a day longer under my roof, and I couldn't blame him for it. The very next morning he set out with his legionaries—and I put my strongest slaves at their side. With almost superhuman effort they managed to fight their way through the man-high snow, all the way from my house to the bridge leading across the Danubius.

Arriving on the south bank, they were spotted by scouts from the legion. The northern wall of the camp borders directly onto the river, and the watchtowers that secure it are manned by soldiers at all hours of the day and night. They recognized Marcellus and sent a strong strike force to meet him, working their way through the snow.

The Celts asked to stay under my roof until they too could return to their homestead. I agreed to their request.

Flamma also stayed. He had decided not to return to Vindobona, but to accompany Morann. Yes, he even spoke of wanting to marry her. The tender love that had blossomed between the two of them in the darkest days seemed to be stronger than any faith, any godly confession.

Neither Morann nor Marcellus made any mention again of the magic remedy against the plague that had originally led Divicia to Vindobona.

I was sure, however, that my friend would come back to it at some point. He was probably confident that he would be able to track Morann down in her secret temple when life got back on track. For now, however, he had had enough of strange gods and their proofs of power, I think.

I could sympathize with him. And I was grateful not to have to travel to a plague-ridden region anytime soon.

As for Caecilia, Marcellus made a decision that I thought was very wise. He did not put her on trial, did not let her suffer an agonizing, sensational death in the arena in front of everyone.

"I cannot have a Christian martyr in Vindobona," he explained to me. Instead, he made a gift of her to a slave trader from the north. He warned the man not to let her come into contact with poisons or herbs and never to turn his back on her.

I never heard of her fate. Did she meet an early death? Or did she spend a long, lonely life of hard labor in the cold lands of the north? Did she ever come to feel remorse for what she had done?

Layla stayed in my house for a few more days—which did not anger Marcellus. He would never have demanded that she fight her way through the ice and snow with him and his men.

At the end of a long day, when the sun had finally come out again, I sat with my beloved Sphinx in the library.

"Layla, I need to ask you something," I began. "Do you remember that night when you thought I was with you? That we had made love, here in the library?"

"Yes?"

"Did you enjoy it?"

For quite a while Layla looked at me in silence, then she said, "I still can't believe it wasn't real."

"But that's not an answer, is it?"

Again she lapsed into silence. "It was different than before," she finally said.

"Different? In what way?"

"I gave myself to you willingly."

"Now listen," I burst out. "You're doing me an injustice. I never forced you to do anything!"

"That is probably true. But you were my master, I was your slave. How many times could I have refused you before you sent me away? Should I not have feared that you would sell me on, to another man who would hardly have been as good to me as you were?"

It was painful to hear these words from her mouth, even though I could understand them.

Instead of reproaching her, I said, "I also had a vision that night, you know. Caused by the kykeon. I had a similar experience as you. I too saw something that concerned the two of us."

Layla looked at me in amazement.

I decided to let her know the whole truth and told her about how Iduna had appeared at the foot of my bed. I gave her the exact words with which my late wife had admonished me: "*Do everything you can to win back Layla's heart. Don't wait until it's too late.*"

I looked Layla firmly in the eyes. "That's what Iduna said to me, as clearly as you are speaking to me now. She also said that you belong to me. That you love me as she once loved me, though perhaps you haven't quite realized it yet. Do you think there could be any truth in that?"

Layla said nothing in reply. She seemed to be deep in

thought.

Finally she raised her head and looked at me from her big black eyes. "Yes, I love you, Thanar. I know that now. And I will never stop loving you. But Marcellus ... my heart belongs to him, too. I don't want to miss him. Oh, I wish I could love like the druidesses!" she cried, seized by sudden passion.

"The druidesses?" I repeated, uncomprehending.

Layla nodded vigorously. "Divicia told me. They do not get married to a man, as is our custom. They remain independent all their lives, and give their hearts and bodies to those they freely choose. One, two, more, the decision is only up to the women. They can love whoever they want for as long as they want, and they don't have to submit to any man. I wish I were one of them—then I could love you both. You and Marcellus."

Do I have to mention that I was speechless? The idea that Layla, following this bizarre rite of the druidesses, would make love to Marcellus or me, depending on her mood, was unbearable to me. Nevertheless, I would probably have welcomed any custom, no matter how strange, if it led Layla back into my arms.

"Iduna, your wife—you lost her to the plague, didn't you, Thanar?" she asked.

I nodded. I had only mentioned it to her once. I never spoke about this loss that was still eating away at my heart, as if I had suffered it only yesterday.

"I, too, was once a wife," Layla said suddenly. "I was married at a very young age, as is the custom among my people. But I loved my husband, couldn't wait to become his bride."

It was the first time she'd told me about a marriage. "What

239

became of your husband?" I asked cautiously. I braced myself for the worst.

"I saw him die. Just like you did with Iduna. Kamani was killed when the slave hunters raided us. That's how I lost my freedom—the same day I became a widow."

I waited, thinking that she would tell me more. But she had nothing to add. She was probably like me; just as I never talked about my wife so as not to torture myself with the memory of her death, Layla had never told me anything about her past. And I had never pushed her to do so.

"Would you like to take a trip to the land of your forefathers?" I asked her after we had been sitting quietly and motionlessly next to each other for quite a while.

The mysterious kingdom of Nubia, from which Layla came, lay south of Egypt. None of my trade journeys had taken me to that part of the world yet, so I hardly knew anything about this country.

Layla shook her head. "I don't want to go back. Nubia is my past. The land of my love for Kamani, whom I have lost irretrievably."

She put her hand on my arm. Her skin was soft and wonderfully warm. "But I would so love to take a greater journey with you someday, Thanar. I hardly know anything of the world. It would make me very happy if you would show me a little of it."

Dramatis personae

Thanar: Germanic merchant with a weakness for Roman lifestyle and culture.

Layla: Thanar's freed slave and former lover, from the legendary kingdom of Nubia. Passionate sleuth and puzzle solver.

Titus Granius Marcellus: legate of the legionary camp of Vindobona.

Severus: a centurion of the Roman legion.
Thessalos: medicus in the legionary camp. Greek.

Divicia: druidess.
Morann: her student.
Granis and Cobanix: Celtic warriors.

Iulius Paulus: Christian apostle, formerly argentarius.
Philomena: his wife.
Caecilia: freedwoman of Paulus.
Flamma: former gladiator.

Enjoyed the book?

Please consider leaving a star rating or a short review on Amazon. Thank you!

More from Thanar and Layla:

GRAND TOUR INTO DEATH
Murder in Antiquity, Book 3

The Germanic merchant Thanar wants to win back the heart of his beloved Layla. What better way to do that than a trip to the Seven Wonders of the World, the favorite holiday destination of the Roman elite?
But death travels with them, and soon Thanar and Layla become entangled in a new murder case—which will make Layla's heart beat much faster than the most beautiful words of love anyway....

More from Alex Wagner:

If you enjoyed *Death of a Preacher Man*, why not try my contemporary mystery series too: *Penny Küfer Investigates*—cozy crime novels full of old world charm.

About the author

Alex Wagner lives with her husband and 'partner in crime' near Vienna, Austria. From her writing chair she has a view of an old ruined castle, which helps her to dream up the most devious murder plots.

Alex writes historical as well as contemporary murder mysteries, always trying to give you sleepless nights. ;)

You can learn more about her and her books on the internet and on Facebook:

www.alexwagner.at/english-books
www.facebook.com/AlexWagnerMysteryWriter

Cover design: Estella Vukovic
Editor: Tarryn Thomas

Made in the USA
Las Vegas, NV
01 March 2024

86570848R00142